SEVENTH-GRADE
WEIRDO

Other Apple Paperbacks
you might enjoy:

The Bad Boys
by Allan Baillie

Wading Through Peanut Butter
Pamela Curtis Swallow

Wizard's Hall
by Jane Yolen

Kidnapping Kevin Kowalski
by Mary Jane Auch

SEVENTH-GRADE WEIRDO

LEE WARDLAW

AN AUTHORS GUILD BACKINPRINT.COM
EDITION

iUniverse, Inc.
NEW YORK   BLOOMINGTON

Seventh-Grade Weirdo

*An Authors Guild Backinprint.com Edition
an imprint of iUniverse, Inc.*

iUniverse books may be ordered through booksellers or by contacting:

*iUniverse
1663 Liberty Drive
Bloomington, IN 47403
www.iuniverse.com
1-800-Authors (1-800-288-4677)*

ISBN: 978-1-4401-8263-1 (sc)

Printed in the United States of America

iUniverse rev. date: 9/29/2009

For Barbara Belli, Dian Regan, Kris Rehler,
and Susie Thomas:
"Some of my best friends are weirdos."

ONE

You've probably read about me. My name is Christopher Robin.

No, not *that* Christopher Robin. I don't own a bear or anything. But I do have a sister named Winnie. That's why you've read about me. I'm the kid with the famous sister. The millionaire sister. The sister who's invented practically the most popular board game in the world. The sister who's only six.

The newspapers have carried articles about her for months. TOY COMPANIES TOAST TALENTED TOT. MINI-GENIUS MAKES MILLION. WHIZ KID WOWS 'EM!

I'd never tell Winnie, but I think the headlines are corny.

"That's because you're consumed with raging jealousy," my best friend, Logan, diagnosed this afternoon. We were in my bedroom, just hanging out because we only have a week of hanging out before school starts. Eighth grade. The kings of Jefferson Junior High. I can't wait.

"Yes, Raging Jealousy," Logan repeated. He made it sound like a disease.

"Uh-huh," I said, only half-listening. I sat at my desk, playing a *Star Trek* game on my computer. The Romulans were closing in. Logan lay on his back in the middle of the floor, crunching his way through a mound of Doritos he had piled on his stomach.

"But don't worry, Rob," Logan continued. *Crunch, crunch.* "There's help for jealous people like you." *Crunch.* "For a small hourly fee, I can counsel you back to your former self. Ten days, max. And maybe a couple of two-day follow-ups."

"I'm not jealous," I said. *Photon torpedoes armed, Captain! Fire when ready, Ensign.* I blasted the Romulan bird of prey, then warped out of the Neutral Zone.

"C'mon, Rob, this is me you're talking to." Logan stood behind me, breathing spicy cheese on my neck. "Who's the guy who ate caterpillars with you in preschool? Who's the guy who braved certain death, belly flopping off the high dive with you in third grade? And last year, when you broke your nose skateboarding, who's the guy who called nine-one-one and tore off his precious NUKE THE WHALES T-shirt for you to bleed on?"

"Mr. Spock?"

"Rob, I don't believe this! We've been through *everything* together, yet you sit there and lie to me about your deepest, darkest feelings."

I heard a choking sound. Glanced over. Logan clutched at his chest, his face a grimace, and keeled backward onto my bed. He flopped around for a few seconds like a beached fish. "I'm wounded, Rob," he panted. "I'm hurt. I'm dying. Truly."

"You're getting mud on my bedspread," I said.

He kicked off his shoes. He had six holes in his socks: four in one foot, two in the other.

"I know you, Rob. Winnie's fame and fortune has got you pea-soup-Christmas-tree-seasick-green with envy. And I don't blame you. I mean, look at this." Logan leapt up and stabbed an article neatly trimmed and tacked on my bulletin board. The headline read KIDDIE PRODIGY KNOWS HOW TO HAVE FUN. "That's gotta be, what, two thousand words written about Super Sis? And not one mention of you."

"Yes, there is. Eighteenth paragraph, last line."

Logan squinted. Then he pushed his nose against the paper. "Oh, yeah. Must've blinked and missed it. *'Winnie Robin lives in Santa Rosita, California, with her parents, John and Nina, and her older brother, Christopher "Rob" Robin, age thirteen.'*" He turned. With one finger he flicked his sunglasses from his head to his nose. "Whoa! I'm dazzled by your star status, man."

I tilted my desk chair so that it balanced on two legs, and folded my arms behind my head. "I'm okay, Logan. Really."

He began to pace. "You're not jealous?"

"No."

"Not a bit?"

"Nope."

"Embarrassed?"

"Naw."

"How about enraged? It doesn't bother you that your sister probably takes money to school for show-and-tell? 'Hello, my name is Winnie,' " he said in a squeaky voice, " 'and today I've brought fifty thousand dollars — in tens and twenties.' "

I had to laugh.

"I mean," Logan continued, "this is so unfair. Winnie just sits back, stuffing monthly checks into her Snoopy lunch box, while we slave away, four afternoons a week, making five dollars an hour *combined*, cleaning swimming pools."

"You know, Winnie hasn't actually earned a million dollars yet," I reminded him. "That's just the estimate from the game company. Besides, my mom and dad are putting Winnie's money into a trust fund. She can't spend any of it without permission till she's twenty-one."

Logan sighed. You could've heard that sigh down the block.

"I gotta go," he announced. "This is depressing." He scooped up his shoes, bookpack, skateboard, and my bag of Doritos, unscrewed the screen, and climbed out the window. Logan likes dramatic exits. Too bad I live in a one-story house.

"See you tomorrow," I said. "Mrs. Rehler's pool. Eight-thirty."

"Yeah." Logan hopped on his skateboard and started to glide away.

He was halfway down the driveway when suddenly, he stopped. "I can't believe you're not even embarrassed," he called. "You've changed, Rob, you know that? You're really *weird*."

"Thanks, Logan."

"I didn't mean it as a compliment!"

"I know, Logan. Good-bye, Logan."

He lifted his shoes in a quick wave.

As I watched him disappear down the street, I thought about what he'd said. He was right. I *had* changed.

Last year, in seventh grade, the last thing I wanted to be was weird. Being ordinary, normal, that was my plan. Which I knew was gonna be hard, because I have the weirdest family in the world, and that kind of stuff is bound to rub off.

But I was determined to be normal like other kids. Normal enough so that I'd blend into the blah-brown walls of the junior high. Normal enough so I'd never get laughed at or picked on. Normal enough to have a few friends, get okay grades, maybe even have a short conversation with a girl. And, I hoped, maybe my normality would miraculously rub off on my family. But things didn't work out that way.

This is the story of my first year in junior high. The year I became the Seventh-Grade Weirdo.

TWO

I woke up the first day of seventh grade with the creepy feeling that someone was watching me.

Usually when I get that feeling, it's because my cat, Steve, is sitting on my chest, staring down at me like Snoopy, playing vulture.

But that morning, Steve wasn't anywhere around.

I lay real still, barely breathing. If a burglar or some guy with a chain saw was nearby, I didn't want him to know that I knew he was there. So without moving my head, I flicked my gaze around the room. Lots of shadows, but bright enough to see that no one was lurking in a corner or behind a chair.

Then I heard it. A rustling sound. Dead ahead.

Cold caterpillars prickled up my neck.

There was someone in my closet.

For a second, I thought it was Steve. Maybe he had pawed open the door a crack and was leaving me an unwelcome surprise. But then I saw them. Two eyes, staring at me from the black depths of jackets and jeans. Brown eyes. Human eyes.

I had to get *them* before they got *me.*

In a flash, I flung back the covers, scooped up my skateboard as a weapon and, with a Ninja cry, wrenched open the closet door.

My five-year-old sister gazed up at me calmly and blinked.

"Winnie!" My voice quivered, half in relief, half in anger. I dropped the skateboard. "Winnie, it's five o'clock in the morning. What are you doing in my closet at *five o'clock in the morning?*"

Winnie blinked again. She was wearing her Winnie-the-Pooh pajamas and sitting on top of my rolled-up sleeping bag. She held a teacup in one hand and a little plate of cookies in the other. In her mouth was Dad's pipe. Not lit, thank goodness.

I lowered my voice to a harsh whisper, so as not to wake up Mom and Dad. "Winnie, answer me!"

Winnie put down the plate and cup and took the pipe out of her mouth. "Good morning!" she said in a British accent. "I'm ever so glad you came to tea. My name is Bilbo Baggins. I'm a hobbit, and this is my hobbit hole. Care for a crumpet?"

My first impulse was to strangle her. I was nervous enough about junior high without starting the morning with a murderer-turned-hobbit in my closet. But sister-strangling wouldn't solve anything. My name and picture would end up splashed across the front page of the newspaper for all the kids to see. That would forever ruin my hopes of blending in, being normal. Besides, with her little pug nose and short brown-bear hair cupped in wispy waves around her face, Winnie was just too cute to strangle.

I sighed and held out my hand. "Come on, Winnie. I'm putting you back to bed. You start kindergarten today. That's a big adventure, so you need your sleep."

Winnie wrinkled her nose. "Adventures are quite annoying. Hobbits don't like adventures, thank you."

"You can't be a hobbit," I said. "Your feet aren't furry."

Winnie glanced down. She was wearing her bear bedroom slippers with the big felt claws, but she didn't argue.

I led her across the hall into her bedroom and tucked her in bed. "Now stay there until seven o'clock. And stay out of my closet *forever*. And give me that pipe!" I whisked it out of her hand.

"Good night, Gandalf," Winnie said.

"Good night, Bilbo," I grumbled and headed back to my room.

I have to explain something here about Winnie. As you may have noticed, Winifred Robin is not your average run-of-the-mill sister. She's a genius. A weird genius.

Up until the age of four, Winnie never spoke a word. Not one syllable. Not even *half* a syllable.

Mom and Dad took her to about twenty-seven doctors, who did a bunch of tests and all came up with the same conclusion. "There's nothing wrong with Winnie," they said. "Her vocal chords are healthy and she has a very high I.Q. Leave her alone, give her time. She'll talk when she's ready."

So Mom and Dad tried to stop worrying.

One morning, not long after her fourth birthday, Winnie wandered into the kitchen and sat next to me at the table. Mom was racing around, crazy as usual, making phone calls, doing laundry, half-dressed, and burning toast.

"Morning, sweetie," she said to Winnie. "Here's your cereal. Eat quick. I'm late."

"Excuse me," Winnie said. "My name is Harriet the Spy and I want a tomato sandwich."

"You're allergic to tomatoes," Mom replied. Then she dropped a quart of milk.

"You talked!" she screamed. "My baby talked!" Mom scooped Winnie into her arms, crying and hugging and squeezing so tight I thought Winnie's eyes would bug out. "The doctors were right. You *can* talk. You can!"

"Doctors are finks," Winnie remarked in disgust.

"They are not!" I said.

"Winnie, Winnie, why haven't you talked before now?" Mom asked, kissing her on the cheeks.

Winnie shrugged. "I didn't have anything to say."

I started to laugh.

"Rob, that's enough." Mom clutched Winnie protectively. "Don't you care that your sister's normal? Aren't you grateful that she can speak?"

"I'm very grateful," I admitted. "All the kids at school have been teasing me for two years about being a brother to the mummy."

"May I have my tomato sandwich now?" Winnie asked. "I have to meet Janie and Sport in half an hour. Janie's going to blow up the world today."

I gave a long, low whistle. "Wow."

"What's she talking about?" Mom cried. "What does it mean?"

"It means," I said, munching my toast, "that Winnie thinks she's Harriet M. Welsch."

"Who?"

I wasn't surprised Mom didn't know what I was talking about. At the time, the only kid's book she had ever read was *Winnie-the-Pooh*.

"Harriet and Sport and Janie are characters from a kid's book called *Harriet the Spy*," I explained. "I know because I just finished reading it last night for school."

"Did you read any parts of the story to Winnie?" Mom asked.

"No."

"Then how . . . ?"

And that's when we realized Winnie had taught herself to read.

It wasn't long before Winnie was reading everything she could get her hands on. Cookbooks, travel books, cereal boxes, encyclopedias. But especially kids' books. And every time she'd read a new one, she'd take on the personality of the main character for a few days. She'd talk like the character, dress like the character, even act like the character. Which got to be a real pain when she'd read stuff like *Curious George* or *Ramona the Pest*.

Winnie's reading skills and character impersonations made her kind of famous. Newspapers all over the country wrote stories about her. She was even on a TV talk show one night, which didn't work out too well. Winnie had just read *Tarzan of the Apes*, and kept calling the host Jane.

Winnie lapped up the publicity like a thirsty kitten, but I hated it. All the kids teased me more than ever. They'd crack stupid jokes like: "Hey, Rob, you gonna sit on your sister's lap tonight so she can read you a bedtime story?" *Har-har.* The only person who didn't give me a bad time was Logan. But then, I guess that's what best friends are all about.

On with my first day of junior high.

After tucking Winnie into bed, I tried to go back to sleep. No luck. First, Dad made all kinds of tromping and humming and grinding-the-beans-for-coffee noises when he got up at five-thirty to go surfing. By then I was wide awake, and my stomach felt funny. One minute it would get tight, like a fist. The next minute, it would zoom through the floor. Just like having my own private roller coaster. Except I knew junior high wouldn't feel anything like Disneyland.

I'd probably forget my locker combination. Even worse, I'd get lost trying to find my first class. Logan and I wouldn't have any classes together. And I could just imagine roll call. Every period, all day long, the other kids would nudge and snicker when the teacher called out —

"Christopher Robin!" Mom's voice jolted me

awake. "Rob, it's seven-thirty. Get a move on!" She pounded on my bedroom door. "Hurry, you're going to be late!"

"Okay, okay," I shouted. I stumbled out of bed and into the bathroom, took the world's fastest shower (24.3 seconds), threw on jeans, T-shirt, and tennis shoes, grabbed my bookpack, and raced into the kitchen.

It was a typical morning at the Robin house. The radio blasted moldy oldies. Kanga and Roo, Mom's parakeets (who are never in their cage), screeched along with the music. Steve and our golden retriever, Piglet, were alternating their woofs and meows in hopes of Meaty Morsels and Chicken Crunchies. Winnie eyed me calmly over her plate of pancakes.

"Hello again, Bilbo," I said.

Winnie gave a regal nod, but didn't answer, her head probably filled with private hobbit thoughts.

The phone rang.

"I'll get it!" Mom called from the other end of the kitchen. The long phone cord wrapped around her like a boa constrictor as she talked and twirled from the stove, to the refrigerator, to the counter where a peanut butter sandwich was half made, to the pad on the wall where she jotted a few notes, and back to the stove to flip pancakes.

Mom is always on the phone. She runs a children's book mail-order business out of our house. She opened it right after Winnie started reading, and now we get calls all day long from people all over the country who want to order books from Mom's catalog. Mom named her company the Heffalump House. You've probably guessed by now that *Winnie-the-Pooh* is her favorite book.

"There's a hobbit in the newspaper today," Winnie said, still speaking in her British accent.

"Really? That's nice, Winnie," I answered, and glanced at the clock. I had four minutes to drink a glass of milk and meet Logan in front of his house. We planned to ride our bikes to school together, as we'd always done since third grade.

"There's a photograph of the hobbit on page one," Winnie continued. "I say, quite a good likeness. And a story about his first day of kindergarten. Hobbits really have no use for school, you know. It's a nasty, disturbing, uncomfortable thing. Makes you late for dinner."

The word *kindergarten* sank in. I almost choked on my milk.

"Let me see that story," I demanded.

Winnie gestured with her fork at the newspaper.

There on the front page was a five-by-seven color photo of my sister. The caption underneath read: *Gifted girl begins school. Is she smarter than her teachers?*

The paper fell to the floor. I must've moaned, because Mom instantly hung up the phone and, still wrapped in its cord, moved to put her hand on my forehead.

"What is it, Rob, are you sick?"

"Yes," I said, pointing at Winnie's picture. "I'm sorry, but I can't go to school. I have to go back to bed. I have to go back to bed and stay there until I'm thirty-three."

Mom laughed. "Honey, no one is going to tease

you about this, believe me. Statistics show that very few junior high students ever read anything, including newspapers. Unfortunately." She began to unwind herself from the phone cord. "Besides," she added, "this is probably the worst thing that will happen to you all day. Isn't it nice to know that it's over and done with?"

"Uh-huh." I slung my bookpack over one shoulder. "I'm going to school now. Good-bye."

"No, wait, stop," Mom said. "Dad left a note. He accidentally ran over your bike this morning when he backed out of the garage."

"What?!" I couldn't believe it. "My BMX is — ?"

Mom nodded. "Totaled. Dad's dropping it off at the bike shop on his way home from surfing."

"Which bike shop?" I asked.

"Umm . . . Bill's Bike and Skate? Does that sound right?"

"Oh, man," I said. "That Bill guy is the slowest in town. My bike won't be fixed until Christmas. Hey, wait a minute. How am I supposed to get to school now?"

"I have to take Winnie to kindergarten," Mom answered, "so I'll drop you and Logan on the way."

I felt that fist in my stomach again. "Uh, that's okay, Mom. Logan and I will just ride our skateboards."

"You are not riding your skateboard six miles," Mom said in her I'm-the-parent-and-you're-not voice. She turned off the stove and hustled Winnie out of her chair. "Come on, sweetie. I'm going to take you and Rob to school in the Heffalump."

She had said it. She had spoken the dreaded H-word.

The Heffalump is Mom's van. It says HEFFALUMP HOUSE in huge, hot-pink letters on three sides. It also has these huge paintings of elephants — plus all the *Winnie-the-Pooh* characters — hopping and lolling and stampeding around, reading books and grinning. When we drive down the road, people just about plow into ditches, they're laughing so hard. And that's the vehicle that was going to drop me smack dab in front of Jefferson Junior High.

Any last hopes I had of starting school a normal person went *thhpptt!* like a deflating balloon. Mom had been wrong when she said the worst was over for that day. I was going to school in the Heffalump. The worst was only beginning.

THREE

How many thirty-seven-year-old mothers do you know who wear ponytails? Or hot-pink velour jogging suits to match their car? Or earrings in the shape of Winnie-the-Pooh with his head stuck in a pot of honey? I know one. Take a guess.

"Move 'em out!" called Mom, her ponytail bouncing and earrings jiggling as she shooed Winnie and me into the van. After we picked up Logan, he and I sat in what Winnie calls the Heffalump Rump — meaning, the third seat, in back. We scrunched real low so no one would spot us as we drove through our neighborhood. We live in a tract where there are about a hundred identical houses, all made of stucco and painted these wild colors. Ours is Pepto Bismol Pink. It gives your eyes a stomachache.

"I have," Logan began in an ominous whisper, "the List."

"What list?" I asked.

"Shhh!" He elbowed me in the ribs. "Reed threatened to tell Mom about me jumping off the roof into the pool if I share this with anyone but you."

Reed is Logan's brother. He's two years older than us and had just started high school.

"What list?" I asked again, only quieter this time.

"*You* know." Logan pulled a three-by-five card from his back pocket. It had stuff written on it in tiny, cramped letters. "This is Reed's *Secrets to Surviving Seventh Grade. Guaranteed to Reduce Stress, Eliminate Worry, and Prepare You for All Major Obstacles — or Your Money Back.*"

"I knew there was a catch," I said. "Okay, how much?"

"Ten bucks."

"Dream on, Logan."

"Okay, okay. For you, seven-fifty."

"Forget it."

"We're talking prime secrets here," Logan insisted. "Five dollars."

"One dollar."

"Sold." Logan grabbed the crumpled bill I dug out of my pocket.

"Does the list say anything about clothes?" I asked. "I don't think the girls are going to let you survive much past second period in that shirt." Logan was wearing a T-shirt that read NO FAT CHICKS.

"What's wrong with my shirt?" he asked in innocence. "People are always commenting on it."

"I'll bet," I mumbled.

"Do you want to hear this or not?" Without waiting for my answer, Logan put on his sunglasses, cracked a few knuckles, cleared his throat, and began to read. I followed along, over his shouder.

Secrets to Surviving Seventh Grade

1. *Don't mess with eighth-graders. If they give you a hard time, go along with it. Act like a wimp. That way, they'll soon get bored, and leave you alone.*

"I demand a refund," I said. "Number one is not a secret. I mean, what does Reed expect? That I'm going to stand up to an eighth-grader like Rambo on the rampage? Come on!"

"Keep reading," Logan said. "You'll get your money's worth. I promise."

2. *Don't — I repeat — don't try to date eighth-grade girls.*

"I'm not planning on dating *any* girls," I said to Logan. "But if I were, what's wrong with an eighth-grade girl?"

"Are you crazy?" Logan replied. "For one thing, she'd be a whole year older than you. A beautiful, self-respecting eighth-grade girl isn't gonna date a seventh-grade guy. They think we're bozos."

"That's nonsense, Rob," Mom called over her shoulder. "I first dated your father when I was fourteen and he was thirteen, and I didn't think anything of it."

She'd been listening!

"Uh, Mom," I began, "don't you think you should be concentrating on your driving?"

She careened around the next corner, tires squealing, as if to spite me. "That's right," she called cheerfully. "Never listen to the wisdom of a mother. We don't know a thing. We were never in seventh grade. We've been completely out of it since Day One."

I shook my head.

"Your mother has a warped sense of humor," Logan remarked.

We scrunched even lower in our seats.

"Any more about eighth-grade girls?" I asked softly.

"Yes. They usually date ninth-graders, which makes the eighth-grade guys mad 'cause then they're left with only seventh-grade girls — who they think are dogs. So if we try to move in on the few eighth-grade girls who don't date ninth-grade guys, the eighth-grade guys will give us a bad time. Got it?"

I worked it through as we stopped at a red light. When the light turned green, I finally understood. "But according to number one," I said, "if we act wimpy, the eighth-grade guys won't give us a bad time. They'll leave us alone."

Logan shook his head. "Number one doesn't work with number two."

"Oh." Seventh grade was more confusing than I'd thought.

3. *Stay away from the lower field. That's where the druggies hang out.*

Number three was no problem. Number three would never be a problem. My life was weird enough without adding drugs to it.

I skipped down to the last "secret" on the list. It was written in dark, bold letters:

4. BEWARE OF THE SHARK

"What's The Shark?" I asked.

"Not 'what,'" replied Logan. "'Who.' The Shark is this kid, Mike Sharkey. Reed was afraid of him last year, and The Shark was only a seventh-grader. He cruises through the halls like a Great White, real cool like, ignoring everybody, just biding his time until — *chomp!*" Logan grabbed me in a headlock and wrestled me to the floor. The Heffalump came to a quick stop.

"We're here, boys," Mom called.

Logan released me and began ripping the three-by-five card into tiny bits. He shoved them into his mouth. "I promised," he said, chewing, "to destroy the evidence."

I sat up and peered out the window. I'd thought we were late, but a bunch of kids were still milling around by the main doors of the school. There was no way they'd miss Logan and me getting out of the Heffalump.

"Hey, Mom," I said. "Wouldn't you like to drive

around the block again? Just until those kids go inside?"

"You're late as it is," Mom answered. "Have a good day."

"But, Mom — "

"Rob, I don't have time for this. I still have to take Winnie to school."

"But, Mom — "

"Rob, if you're not out of the van in five seconds," she announced sweetly, "I shall most certainly blow the horn."

The van is rigged with a special horn. It plays the first eight notes of the *Winnie-the-Pooh* theme song.

"We're going," I said, and grabbed Logan's arm, hauling him over the seat.

"Good-bye, Bilbo." I slid open the door, then ruffled Winnie's hair. "Have fun in kindergarten."

"My name is Alexander," Winnie informed me, "and it's going to be a terrible, horrible, no-good, very bad day."

"Tell me about it," I said, stepping outside.

"Follow my lead," Logan muttered between the clenched teeth of a fake smile. He raised his bookpack in a wave and shouted: "Thanks for the lift, lady! My mom, who got a flat tire this morning, thanks you, too! Sure is lucky you came along!"

"Yeah, right! Thanks for the ride, lady!" I echoed.

Mom gave me a *look*, shook her head, and floored the van out of the parking lot.

Logan and I headed for the main doors. A knot of kids blocked the way. At the center of the knot stood a tall, muscular guy with short, ice-blond hair.

That white hair looked odd with the rest of his face, because he had these thick black eyebrows, and black-black eyes, kind of like bottomless pits. I could tell he was checking us out. He didn't move a muscle, didn't turn his head, but I could feel those eyes boring through us, like laser beams.

"That's The Shark," Logan whispered, whisking off his sunglasses. "Time to wimp out."

I knew Logan was right, but there was something about The Shark's eyes that made me mad, that made me want to stare back at them the same way. I did for a second and got cold. The Shark's eyes were *blank*. Not like a blind man's, but blank like the face plate of a motorcycle helmet. You know, where you don't know who — or what — is behind it.

Quickly, both Logan and I hung our heads and stumbled along. I held my breath, hoping no one would hassle us.

The Shark spoke.

"What kind of weirdo would own a van like *that*?"

I felt my face grow hot.

Logan gave one of his phony nervous laughs and shrugged his shoulders in an I'm-a-wimp-I-don't-know-nothin' gesture.

The Shark looked away. The knot of kids surrounding him loosened to let us pass.

We were going to do it! We were going to escape The Shark!

I didn't see her face, the face of the girl who cut in front of us suddenly, from behind. She had short, dark hair and wore white Reeboks, black socks, a black miniskirt, and a white sweatshirt that read

STAR TREK in black letters across the back. She walked fast. But not fast enough for The Shark to miss her.

She must've been cute, because he said, real smooth: "What's your name, honey?"

"It's Jenner Thomas, sweetie-face," she replied, and kept on walking.

Sweetie-face!

The Shark's face flushed purple.

I couldn't help it. I laughed.

I didn't laugh long. Just long enough to notice that no one else was laughing, that Logan's mouth hung open with shock, and that The Shark's eyes had slid toward me again.

His eyes went *blink-click*, like a camera. I hadn't been on junior high property two minutes, and already I was doomed. The Shark would never forget me now.

FOUR

"Christopher Robin?"

"Here!"

Kids snicker. Whisper.

"Uh, would you please call me Rob?"

"Of course." A smile. The teacher has thought of an original joke. "Say, do you own a bear named—"

"No."

"Were you named after the book—"

"No."

"Any relation to—"

"No."

"Oh. I see. Ahem. All right, where was I? Oh, yes. Cristina Ruiz?"

"Here!"

This scene happened in each of my first three

classes: math, English, and art. Luckily, all the kids in those classes were from other elementary schools in Santa Rosita, so nobody knew I was lying. After the first few giggles, everyone forgot about me and we got down to work. I blend into the scenery, anyway. Despite my weirdo family, I'm an ordinary kid. Ordinary hair (brown, no pink punk-cuts or ponytails), ordinary height (not too tall, not too short), ordinary face. (I couldn't pose for *G.Q.* magazine, but I wouldn't break any mirrors, either.) Grandma thinks I'm cute, but grandmas don't count.

So anyway, the morning went fine. I never got lost, my locker opened on the second try, and not a single eighth-grader hassled me. By fourth period, American history, I was feeling good. Especially when Logan charged through the door, punched my arm, grinned, and chose the desk next to mine.

Then my luck ran out.

"Uh-oh," Logan said in a the-world-is-coming-to-an-end-in-one-minute tone. "Look what the tide just washed in."

I glanced at the door. The Shark stood there, his dark eyes scanning the class like he was looking for tasty morsels to devour. When his gaze met mine, he stopped. His eyes narrowed and he smiled. An evil smile. His teeth flashed as white as his blond hair.

I gulped.

"You're sunk," Logan said. He poked his pencil through a sheet of binder paper, making a white flag. "Quick, Rob, wave this. Unconditional surrender. Mayday, mayday . . ."

Flanked by two of his cronies, The Shark cruised directly toward me. On his way, he knocked his shoulder into a girl, whose books spilled to the floor. "Excuse me," she squeaked. The Shark ignored her. He closed in.

Three desks away . . .

Two desks away . . .

One . . .

Then past me.

Safe!

I let out the breath I'd been holding.

That's when The Shark chose the desk directly behind me. I heard his body sink heavily, ominously, into the seat. Then one crony sat to my right, the other behind Logan, on my left. I was surrounded.

A chill spidered down my neck.

The bell rang, and the door burst open. A tall man with short, curly hair and wide blue-rimmed glasses hustled into the room.

"Good morning, I'm Mr. Wesley," he said, slapping several books and papers down on the lectern. He rolled up his shirt sleeves, crossed his arms, and perched on the edge of his desk. "I'll be teaching you everything you always wanted to know about American history — but were afraid to ask."

Ho-hum, I thought. If the Pilgrims had known how many millions of times we kids would have to study their sea-sickening trip on the *Mayflower*, maybe they never would've left England.

As if he could read my mind, Mr. Wesley said, "Since by now you've probably pigged out on information about Pilgrims and Pocahontas and such, we're going to skip right to the good stuff: the Revolutionary War. Not just boring dates and generals' names. We'll explore important questions such as: What was the philosophy on which this country was founded? How did it differ from that of other countries? And why is it important for you to know this stuff today?"

This sounded more interesting, but I really couldn't concentrate. The Shark had begun to kick my bookpack, which I'd slung across the back of my chair. He used a slow and steady *thunk-thunk-thunk*. Like Chinese water torture. I could feel his eyes singeing my hair.

"... I'll divide the class into eight groups of four," Mr. Wesley was saying. "Starting two months from today, each group will make a twenty-minute oral presentation about some aspect of the war. But please, people. I don't want to see you just standing up here *reading* your reports. Use your imagination." He gave a sharp clap. "Okay, let's take attendance. Then we'll talk more about the presentations."

Mr. Wesley started down the roll sheet. The Shark picked up his kicking pace. I didn't turn around. Just sank lower in my seat. I was determined to obey Reed's instructions, play the wimp, and not let The Shark know he was driving me crazy.

"... Christopher Robin?' Mr. Wesley called.

"Here!"

Kids snickered. Whispered.

"Uh, Mr. Wesley, could you please call me Rob?"

"Of course." He marked something in his book. "Say, Rob, aren't you related to — "

"No."

"You didn't let me finish. Isn't your dad John Robin, the former pro surfer?"

"Well — "

"Of course he is. I just read a piece about him in *Surfer* magazine."

"Oh, how *lame*," The Shark muttered.

"And your sister, Winnie, was in the morning paper," the teacher went on. "Did anyone see this article?"

He snatched a newspaper off the lectern and held it up for the whole world to see.

The Shark snorted.

"Your dad and I went to school together," Mr. Wesley said. "Haven't seen him in years. Man, we had some great times catchin' waves in the old days. Tell him that 'Waterman' Wesley says howzit, all right?"

I stared down at my desk. "Uh, sure."

The kid in front of me turned. "Hey, does your dad wear a bright red wet suit?"

"Yeah," I mumbled. The thing was Day-Glo. It could light up the whole state of Rhode Island.

"I've seen him!" the kid exclaimed."Your dad's the Red Robin! He's the one that rides that gnarly longboard, the kind with only one fin."

The class buzzed. Someone in back started singing *"When the red-red-robin goes bob-bob-bobbing along."* The Shark gave my bookpack such a strong kick, my whole desk shook.

"There ought to be a law," he sneered, "to keep old fogies out of the water. They can't surf worth beans. They're only good as octopus bait."

Octopus bait! I could feel that fist again in my

stomach. Sure, my dad was old (thirty-six), but he surfed great.

"Hey, do *you* surf?" the kid in front of me asked.

"No," I admitted.

He turned away, looking disgusted.

"What's the matter," The Shark said lightly. "Afraid to get your hair wet?"

My face flushed hot as lava, but I still didn't turn around. Not even when I thought I heard the zipper of my pack opening.

"Quiet down, people," Mr. Wesley called. "Say, Rob, I've got an idea. Jefferson is having its Career Day in a few weeks. We invite parents with different kinds of jobs to speak at a student assembly in the auditorium. Do you think your dad would be interested? He could talk about his days on the pro circuit. If I remember correctly, he traveled all over the world and made some good money, too."

Hoo-boy. That's all I needed to totally blow my cover: Dad, standing in front of eight hundred kids, wearing his Day-Glo wet suit and showing slides of the time he went surfing with our *dog.* The same slides that feature me, at age two, running around the beach naked with seaweed on my head.

"Uh, I don't think my dad would qualify for Career Day, Mr. Wesley," I said. "I mean, he's not a pro surfer anymore. He sells real estate now. And, uh, he travels a lot, so he probably won't even be in town then. He sort of has stage fright, too."

"That's not the Red Robin I remember," Mr. Wesley replied with a smile. "Well, listen, ask him for me anyway, will you? You can get back to me about it tomorrow."

I wondered if I could somehow transfer into another American history class. Like, maybe one in Idaho.

Mr. Wesley finished taking attendance. Then he lectured for the next thirty minutes, stopping just before reading time.

"Oh, I almost forgot to assign groups for the ral presentations," he said, taking out the roll book again. "We'll do this alphabetically." He read off a series of names. ". . . and group number eight will be Mike Sharkey, Logan Teplansky, Rob Robin, and Gabriela Vasquez. You'll have a chance to meet with your fellow group members on Friday to discuss topics. After that, you'll meet on your own time. Okay, it's eleven forty-five. Please take out your reading material."

Jefferson Junior High is very big on reading. Every day before lunch, the whole school has to read for fifteen minutes. Not just the kids. *Everybody*: teachers, cooks, janitors, even the principal.

With fumbling fingers, I reached for my pack. The Shark — in *my* history group! The thought was like stepping barefoot into a pool frothing with piranha.

I unzipped my pack and pulled out the latest skateboard mag I'd brought.The mag fell open to a full-color picture of a girl. A *naked* girl. She wasn't even wearing a smile.

"What the — ?" I slammed shut the magazine. There were two equally naked girls on the cover. Big, bold letters informed me that I held the anniversary edition of *Nudie News*.

"Rob!" Logan had leaned into the aisle to get a

better look. He clucked his tongue. "Rob, I'm shocked!"

"Shut up," I muttered through clenched teeth. "This isn't mine. I don't know where it came from." Then I remembered The Shark and the unzipping noise I'd heard.

I whirled to face him. "You!" I said. He stared at me blankly over the top of *my* skateboard mag. "You switched magazines! Give mine back. Now."

Logan cupped a hand around his mouth and mumbled, "Ex-nay, Rob. Ex-nay."

The Shark just smiled. "Don't you *like* looking at pictures of naked girls, Christopher Robin? Oh, I see. You prefer pictures of naked *bears*."

I opened my mouth to call The Shark a name that would've sentenced me to fifteen-years-to-life if repeated at home.

A firm hand clapped down on my shoulder.

"Do you have a problem, gentlemen?" Mr. Wesley asked.

"Yeah," said one of The Shark's cronies. "Rob brought a nudie magazine to school."

"No — I — but — " I sputtered.

Mr. Wesley made a gesture for silence. Then he held out his hand. "May I?"

I handed over the magazine.

He riffled through several pages."Hmmm. You know, Rob, this is supposed to be a reading period. I'm afraid I don't see a whole lot of reading material in this magazine."

"You could use it for reading Braille," The Shark suggested.

The class snickered.

Mr. Wesley closed the magazine, crossed his arms, and stared down at The Shark. "Mr. Sharkey," he began, "I can't tell you how sincerely happy I am that you've joined my class . . . for the second time. I'm sure we'll have another interesting year together." Mr. Wesley shifted his attention to me. "Okay, Rob, let's hear your side of the story first. Is this, or is this not, your magazine?"

I shook my head. "No, it isn't. I brought a skateboard mag. I think he" — I jeked a thumb over my shoulder — "stole it, and planted the nudie mag in my bookpack."

"Can you prove this?" Mr. Wesley asked.

I plucked the magazine out of The Shark's hands. "Sure. See this mailing label on the front? This is me. And my address."

The teacher nodded. "I see. Mike Sharkey, may I speak to you outside for a moment?"

The Shark heaved a huge sigh, but stood to follow Mr. Wesley. As he passed my desk, he lowered his face so we were eye to eye. "Snitch," he hissed. "You're really gonna eat it now." Then he sauntered out the door.

The whole class was silent. They stared at me, their mouths hanging open.

"Oh, Rob," Logan moaned. "Man, what have you *done*?"

FIVE

Something weird hap-
pened to me during sixth period. Weirder than anything else that happened that day.

At first, I thought I had the flu. My mouth got dry,
as if I'd just eaten a bowl of Shredded Wheat —
without any milk. I got flashes of hot and cold. Then
my stomach started doing loop-de-loops. I wasn't
sick, though.

Just in love.

It happened halfway through science class. Logan and I lucked out and were in another class
together. We chose seats in the back row and were
busy copying assignments off the blackboard when
the guy from the A.V. department came in to set
up the film projector. Except it wasn't a guy. It was

the girl in the STAR TREK sweatshirt. The one who had called The Shark sweetie-face. Jenner Thomas.

"Hey, Rob," Logan said. "Are you all right?"

I couldn't answer. My tongue weighed three hundred pounds. Jenner wheeled the projector down the aisle and stopped one seat in front of me, to my right. I could've touched the hem of her skirt.

"Would you like something to drool into?" Logan asked.

Jenner was beautiful. Tall and thin, with short, black-brown hair that looked like she'd been out in a breeze. She wore tiny, gold-hooped earrings that peeked from underneath her hair. She was very tan, with freckles, and her lips curved up in the corners. I loved her eyes the best. Lime green. Not like popsicles or Jell-O, but that black-green shade that real limes are.

"I could call the paramedics," Logan offered.

I watched her thread the projector. She had quick hands and short, neat nails, not bitten (like mine). Our science teacher darkened the room, and Jenner started the film. I was very impressed. She was an expert at her job. Never once did the picture get out of frame. Even when the film broke, she instantly rethread it with an easy *click, flick, snap.* After that, she rested her hand on the projector like she owned it, like it couldn't run without her. And it probably couldn't.

"Do you need mouth-to-mouth?" Logan whispered. "Not that *I'm* offering, or anything."

I don't remember what the film was about. I

watched Jenner's silhouette the whole time. I got to know the shape of her nose, the way her lashes turned up on the ends. I liked the way she stood there real cool, without knowing she was cool at all. I wondered about her name.

The film ended. Lights flooded the room. I blinked, feeling like a possum, frozen in the headlights of a car.

Jenner rewound the film and placed it in its cannister. She unplugged the projector and coiled the cord. She was ready to leave. She was going to walk away. I had to say *something* . . .

I swallowed against the Shredded Wheat. "Nice work." The words came out a croak.

Jenner raised an eyebrow and one side of her mouth in a quick smile. "Thanks," she said.

I watched her start down the aisle. She had talked to me! She had said *thanks*! This could lead to bigger and better things, like saying hi in the halls. Then, one day, her locker would get stuck. I could offer to open it. She'd be so grateful, she'd ask me to eat lunch with her. We'd talk about *Star Trek*. I'd invite her over some afternoon to watch it. No, no. That way she'd have to meet my family. No, she'd invite me over to *her* house, and then . . .

"Earth to Rob, Earth to Rob." Logan's voice shattered my thoughts.

"What?" I said crossly.

"Forget her," he replied.

"Forget who?" I asked, trying to sound casual.

"Her. *Her*." Logan pointed at Jenner's back. "Are you crazy, Rob? Don't you remember number two

· 35 ·

of *Secrets to Surviving Seventh Grade*? Jenner is an *eighth*-grader!"

"Oh." Every bone in my body turned to spaghetti. I slumped in my seat and watched as Jenner wheeled the projector — and herself — out of my life.

SIX

After school, Logan's mom took us home. What a relief. My first day of seventh grade had seemed longer than a visit to the dentist. The kind of visit where you get six cavities filled.

"Hello, Rob," my parents chorused when I walked in the back door. They were both working at the kitchen table.

"Hi," I answered. That set off a chain reaction.

Piglet bounded to greet me, barking his head off . . .

Which woke up Steve, who leapt off the top of the refrigerator where he'd been sleeping . . .

Which startled Kanga and Roo, who started screeching like someone was hacking their wings off . . .

Which made Mom and Dad look at each other and burst out laughing.

Sometimes I wish my parents didn't work at home. I wouldn't mind being a latchkey kid. How neat to come into a house that's empty and quiet and *normal*.

Still chuckling, Mom turned back to her computer, which she keeps at one end of the kitchen table. She must've been logging in a new shipment of children's books. There were piles and piles of them toppling everywhere. Dad sat at the other end of the table, tap-tapping something into *his* computer.

"Nina," he said to Mom, "remember that huge house I listed last week? The one I couldn't think of a catchy ad for? Well, listen to this." He cleared his throat. "The headline is, SPACE: THE FAMILY FRONTIER. Under that I have: STOP YOUR EXPLORATION! YOUR TREK TO FIND A SPACIOUS HOME WILL END WHEN YOU WARP YOUR WAY TO THE ROOMIEST HOUSE THIS SIDE OF THE MILKY WAY. What do you think?"

"Fine, dear, just fine," Mom murmured.

"What do you think, Rob?" Dad asked.

I had a feeling the ad would only appeal to Klingons, but I said, "Great, Dad, just great."

"Good. I'm stoked about it. Say, I wonder if it should read instead, BEAM ABOARD THE ROOMIEST HOUSE THIS SIDE OF ALPHA CENTAURI. Hmmm. This might be another award-winner."

I don't know if Dad's ads ever bring in new clients, but our kitchen walls are lined with little gold plaques he's won. They were awarded by the real estate company he works for. The plaques all say IN RECOGNITION FOR MOST CREATIVE ADVERTISING, which I think really means MOST WEIRD.

I scratched Piglet behind the ears for a moment to distract him from slobbering on my shoes, then opened the refrigerator to get a soda.

"Mom," I said, "there are three picture books in here next to the juice. Are they hibernating or something?"

"Oh, *that's* where those are." She frowned without looking up from her work. "I wondered why the package of bacon was sitting on the coffee table. Take them out, will you?"

"Sure."

"So, Rob," Dad said, finished with his ad. "Tell me, what was the most awesome thing that happened to you today?"

That's something I like about Dad. He never asks stupid questions you can't answer, like "How was school?" or "What did you learn?" I only wish he wouldn't use that surf slang. A dad should talk like, well, like a *dad*.

I opened a Coke and took a gulp, thinking about Dad's question. My mind flashed on Jenner, until I remembered I was supposed to forget her. "I guess the most awesome, I mean the best thing that happened," I answered, "is that Logan and I have two classes together."

Dad nodded. "Radical. Safety in numbers, you know. And what's the worst thing that happened? Wait — don't tell me." He closed his eyes and put a hand to his forehead like a mind reader. "You're sharing a gym locker with a King Kong look-a-like who doesn't wear deodorant. No, no — your art teacher is into modern art and you spent the entire morning drawing pictures of headless chickens. No, that's not bad enough. I know! Some moron of a father ran over your bike . . . for which he is really and truly sorry."

I looked down at my shoes. "That's okay, Dad."

"No, it isn't, Rob. You worked months cleaning all those swimming pools to earn half the money for that bike, and I destroyed it with one swift *crunch*."

I winced. Dad is good at special effects noises.

"Admit it," Dad said. "I'm a bozo. It's all right. I won't get offended. Raise your right hand and repeat after me: *My father is a bozo*."

I laughed, but did as I was told. "My father is a bozo."

"My father is a nerd."

"My father is a nerd."

"My father couldn't drive his way out of a paper bag, but I will, eventually, forgive him because deep down he's basically a nice guy who pays all the bills —"

"Half the bills," put in Mom.

" *— half the bills*," continued Dad, *"and is even pretty good-looking, which is more than can be said of most fathers."*

"Uh, right," I said.

Dad grinned. "Aside from paying for all the repairs, what do you think my punishment should be, Rob?"

I took another sip of Coke. "You could take my kitchen duty for the next two weeks," I offered.

"Cowabunga, Rob! That's highway robbery!"

"Okay. Ten days."

"Eight days and you got a deal." Dad held out a hand.

I shook it and said, "I'm gonna skateboard over to Bike and Skate now. I want to check if that Bill guy started work on my bike."

"Fine, go ahead," Mom answered. "But take Winnie with you."

I gave her what I thought was my biggest pained look. "Do I *have* to?"

"Yes, you do."

"Mom, please don't make me." I scooped a pile of books off a chair and thudded into the seat. "The last time I took Winnie somewhere, she recited the first chapter of *Charlie and the Chocolate Factory* in the middle of the sidewalk. She was wearing that ratty T-shirt she loves, and people thought we were homeless kids and started throwing money."

Mom bit her lip, trying not to laugh. Her ponytail quivered.

"Just once," I said, "I wish she'd act like a regular kid and talk in her own voice. Except I don't even know what that voice is, because she's always too busy being somebody else!"

"Rob — "

"I'm not taking her," I insisted. "She's embarrassing. She's weird."

"She's your *sister*," Mom said. "And right now she could use a little brotherly support. Winnie had a rough time in school this morning."

I thought back on *my* day. "What kind of rough time can you have in kindergarten?" I asked. "Choosing between red or green for finger painting?

Which thumb to suck at rest time?"

Mom fingered a Pooh earring. "Winnie does fine in front of TV cameras and interviewers, Rob, but kindergarten was another matter altogether. Kids teased her. Refused to play with her. Her teacher insisted she couldn't handle a "genius," so mid-morning, the principal transferred Winnie to another class. Winnie was literally *trembling* when I brought her home."

Poor Winnie. Yet I couldn't help thinking she deserved it. If she'd acted normal like the other kids, none of this would've happened.

"Your dad and I spent some time with her after lunch," Mom went on, "but we both have work to do now. It would be such a big help if you . . ."

"Okay, okay," I agreed, knowing the argument was lost. "Where is she?"

"In her room," Dad said. "Thanks, Rob."

"Uh-huh." I made a path through the jungle of books that tangled the living room floor, then trudged into Winnie's bedroom. Not there. Probably playing in the backyard, in her sandbox. I'd look for her when I was ready to go.

In my room, I put on my favorite skating T-shirt, grabbed my skateboard, and opened the closet to get a jacket.

"Hello," said a voice at my feet.

I almost dropped the skateboard. "Winnie!" I clutched my chest. "You scared me to *death*! What are you doing in my closet? I thought I told you to stay out of my closet forever!"

"My name is Alexander," Winnie said, "and I'm having a terrible, horrible — "

" — no good, very bad day," I finished for her. "I know. So am I. Please stop reminding me."

Winnie blinked. She was crouched on top of my sleeping bag again, arms hugging her legs, chin resting on her knees. "At school," she began in Alexander's voice, "no one wanted to be my buddy for field trips, the hamster peed on my hand, I stubbed my toe during recess, and I had to carry a snack in my Snoopy lunch box. I hate my Snoopy lunch box."

I sighed. My life felt like a TV rerun. Hadn't I done this before? "Come on, Winnie," I said, holding out a hand. "Let's get out of here."

"Where are we going?" she asked, slipping her cold hand into mine.

"Australia."

Bill's Bike and Skate shop is only about a mile from our house, but I never go there. That's because the place is a pit. There's always dust all over the counters and skateboards, and cobwebs in the spokes of the bikes. The same T-shirts and posters have been hanging on the walls since the Civil War. Bill, the owner, might be a good mechanic, but nobody knows for sure. From what I've heard, Bill's so slow and lazy, he's never finished work on anything.

When Winnie and I walked in, the little bell above the door jangled for a second, then plunged to the floor with a clang. Bill didn't even look up. He was sitting on a stool, reading a newspaper, his feet resting on the counter.

"With you in a sec," he drawled.

Winnie picked up the rusty bell that had fallen, and we made our way to the counter. We were the only customers in the shop. The place was dark and so quiet, I felt like I was in a library. A very dirty library. The air smelled like rubber tires and greasy bicycle chains. I think Bill used the same grease to comb his blond hair. There was a lot of it on his T-shirt, too.

After about five minutes, Bill finally finished reading his newpaper. "Can I help you," he said. It was a statement, not a question, and he looked like he didn't want to help us at all.

I cleared my throat. "My dad, John Robin, brought in a bike this morning," I said. "I want to find out when you think it'll be ready."

"Soon," Bill replied, and picked up his paper again.

"How soon?" I asked.

"When I say soon, I mean soon."

"But — "

Bill heaved a huge sigh. "Look, kid, I got a lot on my mind these days, see? Business isn't so hot. It's hard to work when ya got money troubles, ya know?"

I was about to point out that he wouldn't have money troubles if he worked once in a while, when I heard the door open behind me.

I turned and froze.

The Shark. And two of his cronies. They were wheeling in a bike.

I whipped behind a huge, cardboard cut-out of a skateboarder, hoping they hadn't seen me. Winnie stared at me curiously and blinked. I put a finger to my lips.

"Hey, Bill," The Shark said. "The stupid chain fell off my bike again. I need it fixed right this time, and I need it fixed now."

"I'll get to it soon," Bill replied.

"Not soon. *Now.*"

Bill straightened quickly. "Okay, okay," he said. I thought I heard his voice tremble. Geez, was *everybody* afraid of The Shark?

"Christopher Robin," Winnie demanded in her British accent, "what are you doing back there? Is Tigger with you?"

I made a slashing motion across my throat, but Winnie just looked confused.

"Christopher Robin?" The Shark asked. I could hear the evil smile in his voice. "Is Christopher Robin really here, in person, up close, and personal?"

Rats. No use hiding now. I stepped from behind the cut-out.

"Well, well," The Shark said, sugary-sweet. "And look, guys, he's got the famous Winnie-the-Pooh with him."

"So, uh, um," I stuttered at Bill, "you say my bike will be ready soon?"

"Yeah, soon," Bill said.

"Great. Let's go, Winnie." She tiptoed to put the rusty bell on the counter, then took my hand.

The Shark stood in our way. "So, this is the genius, huh?" he asked, circling us to get a better look. His bicycle chain dangled from one hand, dancing like a marionette. "You don't look too bright to me, little girl. Go ahead. Say something smart."

Winnie blinked at him. "I will when you do," she said.

The Shark glared at her.

"Hey," Bill broke in, peering closer at Winnie. "You're *her*. That kid genius in the paper. See? Right here." He tapped a long, bony finger at the front page.

Winnie ignored him. "Shall we go, Gandalf?" she asked. "It's almost time for tea. I baked two nice seedcakes for us at home."

The Shark and his cronies hooted.

"You've got a gold mine here, Christopher Robin," The Shark said. "You could sell this kid to the circus for a ton of money. She'd fit right in with the dog-faced boy, the bearded woman, and all the other freaks." He snapped his fingers. "Yeah, you could tour as an act! Presenting, the Midget Genius and the Seventh-Grade Weirdo."

"Shut up," I muttered.

The Shark cupped a hand to his ear. "*What* did you say to me?"

"I said, shut up."

The Shark chuckled. "Did you hear that guys?" he asked, smirking at his friends. "The Seven-Grade Weirdo wants *me* to shut up."

Without warning, The Shark snapped around and shoved me with both hands. I stumbled backward, hitting my head on the counter, and slid to the floor. Little stars appeared in front of my face, just like in the comics. Tears stung my eyes.

"Hey, hey, none of that in here," Bill shouted, "or I'll call the cops."

"No, you won't," The Shark said in an icy-calm voice. "But don't worry. I'll deal with the Seventh-Grade Weirdo another time. We're in the same little history group, remember, Christopher Robin?"

He laughed and tossed his chain on the counter. "I'll be back to get my bike in an hour, Bill. It'd better be ready." The Shark and his cronies cruised away. The door slammed with a bang.

Winnie crouched down and peered into my face, her eyes wide. "Are you hurt, Gandalf?" she asked.

I didn't answer. I stood up slowly, massaging the throbbing bump on my head. My throat ached from trying not to cry. I looked down. My favorite T-shirt now had two greasy handprints forever tatooed on the front.

"We're leaving," I said, my voice coming out hoarse. I stumbled out the door. Winnie scampered behind me.

"Are you hurt, Gandalf?" she repeated when we reached the street.

"Don't call me Gandalf," I yelled. "And don't ask stupid questions. Of *course* I'm hurt. And it's all your fault. Look what happened. My shirt is ruined, I've got a bump on my head the size of Ohio, and now The Shark hates me more than ever. And all because of *you!*"

Winnie blinked at me. I saw a tear slip down her cheek.

"Oh, I'm sorry, Winnie," I said, brushing the tear

with my thumb. "Don't cry. And don't look at me like that. It's just that sometimes — oh, never mind. I'm sorry. Come on, let's go home. I didn't mean what I said."

But deep down, I knew I really did.

SEVEN

The next few days were normal, or as normal as my life ever gets.

Dad drove Logan and me to school every day in his faded, rusty 1968 VW van. It stalls at traffic lights, doesn't have a reverse, smells like surf wax, and is covered with decals that say things like LIFE'S A BEACH and I'D RATHER BE SURFING — but at least it's less embarrassing than the Heffalump.

Mom got five more shipments of children's books for the pre-pre-Christmas rush, and ran out of places to store them. The piles in the living room got higher and higher until they looked like miniature Leaning Towers of Pisa. If any more arrived, we'd be using them as place mats.

Winnie became the mouse character Mrs. Frisby and tried to organize the other kindergartners into a revolutionary group called the Rats of NIMH. Mom never told me any details, but Winnie's teacher quit that afternoon, probably suffering from the early stages of a nervous breakdown. The principal transferred Winnie to the third and last kindergarten class.

At school, things went okay. Logan and I got used to having seven different teachers, only two classes together, and eating bizarre stuff in the cafeteria, like Rubber Pizza, Crunchy Fish Surprise, and Beef Stew with UFOs (unidentified floating objects).

I caught a couple of glimpses of Jenner in the halls. And once, at lunch, I watched her out of the corner of my eye for almost five minutes. She sat, two tables away, with a group of other eighth-graders. She was laughing and gesturing with a sandwich, her little gold earrings sparking under the fluorescent lights.

I knew I shouldn't look at her. I knew I should forget her. But I couldn't. She was like a bruise. The kind that turns those swirly blue and green colors that are so fascinating, you have to touch it — even though you know it's going to hurt.

And then, of couse, there was The Shark.

I expected him to do all sorts of horrible things to me. I don't know exactly what. I figured he had this extra piece of brain labeled INDESCRIBABLY HORRIBLE AND TORTUROUS THINGS TO DO TO PEOPLE I HATE. But Tuesday passed, and Wednesday, and Thursday, too, and nothing happened.

"Maybe The Shark's still digesting the last seventh-grader he ate," Logan said. "Just keep acting wimpy, and by the time he's ready to feed again, he'll have forgotten all about you."

I knew better. The Shark was just waiting. I could feel it in those black, blank eyes as they laser beamed into my skull, sending hot chills down my back during Wesley's class. The Shark was going to get me. I just didn't know when. Or how . . .

"Rob," Mr. Wesley began in class on Friday, "did you get a chance to ask your dad about Career Day?"

Rats. I had hoped Wesley wouldn't remember that stupid day. "Uh, um, no," I mumbled into my shirt collar.

"What was that? Speak up, please."

"Um, no. I forgot." Not really a lie. I *had* forgotten. On purpose.

"Well, I think I'll give him a call myself," Mr. Wesley said. "The program's scheduled for the end of the month, and we need one more parent. You're listed in the phone book, aren't you? Great." He made a note to call Dad. I made a note to be allergic to school on Career Day.

"All right, people." Mr. Wesley clapped his hands. "Get into your presentation groups, please."

There were a lot of scuffling and scooting noises as people played musical chairs. Gabriela Vasquez dragged her desk over between Logan's and mine.

"Make a circle, you guys," she instructed.

Logan and I glanced at each other and sighed. I still couldn't believe The Shark was in our group. We turned our desks to face him. He didn't look at us. He was sharpening a pencil with his teeth.

"I think we should have a chairperson," Gabriela began. "Any volunteers?"

Logan obviously wanted to impress her. He cleared his throat and touched his fingertips together. "I'm told by those in the know," he said in a deeper than usual voice, "that I'm extremely well organized. I also interface well and am proficient in dealing with innovative theories."

Gabriela gave him an exasperated look. "What?"

His "intelligence" wasn't working. Next, Logan tried charm. "You're cute," he said, cocking his head and grinning. "I nominate *you*."

Give it up, Logan, I thought. Gabriela was wearing a pink T-shirt that read in curly letters CATS ARE PEOPLE, TOO. Logan's shirt had a green, slimey Gila monster on the front. It said: ALIEN SKATEBOARD MUTANT FOR PRESIDENT. Logan and Gabriela would never hit it off.

Gabriela took out a piece of binder paper and neatly wrote across the top: *First Meeting*. "Okay, I'll be the chairperson, if no one objects — " She glanced at me. I shook my head. She glanced at The Shark. He had finished his pencil snack and was now writing on his desk. He shrugged a shoulder. "Well, that's settled," Gabriela went on. "I have some ideas, anyway."

She told us how her family had gone East on vacation that summer, and spent a lot of time in Concord, Massachusetts. "That's where the first big battle of the Revolutionary War was fought," she explained. "I was thinking that for our presentation, we could pretend to go back in time to Concord and interview British and American soldiers. You know, ask them why they're fighting and what it's like and stuff."

"Excellent," Logan said, nodding. "You have a keen mind."

Oh, brother, I thought. But it *was* a good idea. "Hey, why don't we make it like a real TV news show?" I suggested. "One of us could be an anchorperson and read news about the war like it's happening today. Then we could go 'live,' behind the scenes, and interview the soldiers and townspeople, maybe even famous guys like Paul Revere."

Gabriela leaned forward. "Hmmm . . . yeah, that's good, Rob. What do you think, uh . . . Mike?"

The Shark glared at her for a split second from under dark eyebrows, then concentrated on his desk again. I couldn't make out what he'd written, but the letters were at least two inches high and three-dimensional. The Shark shaded them with heavy, black strokes.

Gabriela took a deep breath. "Well. Any more ideas?"

We — or, at least, Logan, Gabriela, and I — talked about the "show" for the next few minutes, then agreed to meet Monday, after school, to start writing our script.

"I know I'm chairperson, but we can't meet at my house," Gabriela apologized. "My parents work, and I'm not supposed to have friends over when no one else is home."

"Wow, we have something in common!" Logan said. He shook his head sadly. "Aren't parents just *awful*?"

Gabriela didn't answer. She looked at The Shark. "Can we meet at your house, Mike?"

"No way." He never took his gaze off his desk.

"Rob?" Gabriela asked.

No way, I thought, silently echoing The Shark's words. No way could I let that happen. The Shark would see my parents, and Kanga and Roo, and Piglet, and the Heffalump, and he'd make nasty remarks again about Winnie, and —

"No problem," Logan said, relaxing back in his chair. "Rob's parents are always around. And they won't mind, will they, Rob? Oh, and come hungry. Mr. Robin bakes the best coconut macaroons."

The Shark snickered.

"How are things coming?" Mr. Wesley asked suddenly from behind me. He'd been making his way around the class, checking on each group.

"We've got a good idea, Mr. Wesley," Gabriela said. "And we're going to meet at Rob's house on Monday."

Mr. Wesley nodded. "I'm glad to see you're not putting this off until the last minute." He moved behind The Shark and laid a big hand on his shoulder. "And remember, since this is a group presentation, each one of you will have to do your share. That means committing one hundred percent. Right, Mr. Sharkey?"

The Shark had covered his desk with his hands. "Of course, Mr. Wesley," he replied. "Don't worry about me. When I commit to something, I never let it go." He stared right into my eyes and smiled. That evil smile.

I didn't quite understand what he meant until after class. As he and his cronies cruised out the door, I took a peek at his desk. In those black, three-dimensional letters The Shark had written: DEATH TO THE SEVENTH-GRADE WEIRDO.

EIGHT

I knew The Shark wasn't really going to kill me. But some things are worse than death. I found that out during seventh period.

"Okay, number off for teams!" Mr. Hernandez, the P.E. teacher, shouted after the class suited up. "Touch football today. Yeah, I know it's hot, but I wanna see a little action out there!" He blew his whistle. "Okay, let's go!"

We trotted out onto the field and lined up for the kickoff. We played for a half hour, breaking into huddles now and then to discuss moves and positions. I think we did more clapping and shouting and backslapping than making any yards, but we had fun. Then Mr. Hernandez called a time-out. We stood, breathing hard, squinting at him in the bright sun.

"Switch positions for a while," he instructed, "so you get a better feel for the game." He glanced at a clipboard. "Justin, I want you as quarterback for Team A. Rob, you switch to center for the B's."

I nodded and bent to reknot my shoelaces.

"Oh, and we've got a substitution," Mr. Hernandez continued. "Mike here has just transferred from another class and wants to get in some playin' time before the period's over. I'm puttin' him on Team A as a middle linebacker. Okay, let's do it!" He blew another sharp blast on his whistle.

I finished my shoes and straightened. Directly across from me stood The Shark.

"Hello, Weirdo," he said softly.

I swallowed. It felt like a gym sock had been stuffed down my throat.

"Hut-hut-hut!" the quarterback called behind me.

My hands were trembling, but I hiked the ball. It sailed clean over the quarterback's head.

Team A cracked up.

"Easy does it, Rob," Mr. Hernandez yelled. "Try that again."

The quarterback tossed me the ball. "It's okay, man," he said, though his lips were tucked down with irritation.

"How's your gnarly surfin' dad?" The Shark asked cheerfully. "What's his cute nickname again? Oh, yeah, Birdbrain Robin."

My stomach clenched as tight as my teeth.

"Hut-hut-hut!"

I snapped the ball with ferocious speed. It hit the ground and bounced into the quarterback's nose.

Team A cracked up again.

My face burned with embarrassment.

"No, no, no, Rob," Mr. Hernandez shouted, waving his arms around. "You're not concentrating. Stay cool. Use control. Try again. Third time's a charm, right?"

The quarterback smacked the ball into my stomach. His nose was the color of a candy Red Hot. "Get with it, Rob," he growled.

I nodded, then wiped my hands on my jersey. Sweat trickled down the side of my face. I turned toward The Shark again.

"How's dear Winnie-the-Pooh?" he asked in a honey-dripping voice.

"Shut up," I muttered, falling back on the old standby. I'd probably think of a snappy comeback on March 10, two A.M.

"I'll bet Winnie got you a hot date for the weekend," The Shark went on. "Little Bo Peep, perhaps?"

"Hut-hut-hut!"

I threw down the ball and slammed into The Shark, knocking him over. He made an *ooomph* sound, and we tumbled to the ground. I landed on top. I wanted to make his nose reversible with my fist, but the wind had been knocked out of me. I lay there gasping while kids hooted and yelled.

A strong arm yanked me to my feet. "Break it up, break it up," Mr. Hernandez shouted. He didn't have to worry. I didn't have enough breath to blow over a toothpick.

"You saw it, everybody saw it," The Shark said, his words coming out fast but cool. "The weirdo came at me for no reason, no reason at all."

Everybody nodded and said, "Yeah — we saw it, yeah." One kid muttered, "Geez, I think Rob lost a few tiles on reentry." I couldn't argue. I was bent over, hands on my knees, catching my breath.

"Rob, that was inexcusable," Mr. Hernandez said. "I don't know what your problem is, but I don't ever want to see that kind of poor sportsmanship again. Ten laps around the field. *Now.* The rest of you, hit the showers!" He blasted his whistle.

The whole class charged toward the locker room. All except The Shark. He got to his feet and then, as if I weren't there, took his time plucking bits of grass off his jersey. I glared at him, trying to put three tons of hate into my expression. Finally, our eyes locked. The Shark didn't flinch. He just lifted one black eyebrow like Mr. Spock, flashed me his evil smile, and cruised back to the gym.

Still out of breath, I set off, stumbling, on my first lap around the field.

It took twenty minutes to finish the run. By the time I straggled back, I had a stitch in my side and school had ended. The locker room was deserted. It smelled like sweaty shoes, wet towels, and steam.

I stripped off my shirt and shorts, grabbed a towel, and headed for the shower. All the hot water was gone, but the cold felt pretty good. I ducked my head under the faucet and let the water pound down on me. I stayed that way for a few minutes, repeating over and over all the curse words I'd ever heard in my life. Then I made up a few. They all fit The Shark perfectly.

I glanced at my watch. Late. Logan and his dad

would be waiting for me in the parking lot. I had to hurry.

Hitching the towel around my waist, I scooted back to my locker. I didn't remember leaving it unlocked. So why was the door standing open? Then I noticed the lock had been smashed. I glanced inside.

Empty. Completely empty. My clothes, my gym stuff, my shoes, my bookpack — everything was gone.

The Shark.

I let out a Ninja cry and kicked my locker as hard as I could. My foot felt like it had been run over by a Mac truck. I hopped around, holding it, and used some of my brand-new curse words. That made me feel a little better, until I realized that underneath my skimpy towel, I was stark naked.

I'd have to see if Mr. Hernandez could help. Maybe he could call my mom and have her bring me some stuff from home.

I limped out of the locker room to his office, leaving a trail of wet footprints behind me. The *slap-slap* of my feet echoed eerily in the dim, deserted hall. When I got to his door, I knocked twice. No answer. I tried the handle. Locked.

Mr. Hernandez had left for the day.

Nobody knew I was there except — The Shark.

My heart squeezed with panic. I couldn't leave school wearing only a towel. I might get arrested. What if I had to spend the whole night there?

Then I heard faint voices, coming from the gym. I breathed a sigh of relief. Somebody was still around.

I hobbled down the hall and pushed open the gym doors. "Hey," I called — and froze.

Fifteen girls in leotards stopped their somersaults to stare at me.

"EEEEEeeeek!" screamed one girl. "A pervert!"

"I know him," said another. "I know that pervert. He's in my history class."

"Hey, let's see what you look like without that towel, cutie!"

Giggles, snickers, pointing fingers.

Somebody made a low, strangled sound. *Me.* Clutching my towel, I slammed the door. My face felt like a roasted marshmallow.

Where now? I started to my right, down another shadowy hall. At the far end, the outside door opened. In a square of sunlight, I saw the silhouette of The Shark. He and his two cronies were coming my way. My heart pounded like machine-gun fire. Who knew what they had planned for me now? I didn't want to hang around long enough to find out.

Ignoring the pain in my foot, I sprinted back the way I'd come and flung open the first door I came to.

I smashed it shut behind me, locked it, and turned around. I was in a conference room filled with trophy cases. At the far end, rewinding a film in a projector, stood Jenner.

I closed my eyes and wished to be struck by lightning. Or an 8.6 earthquake. Maybe both.

"Don't — don't worry," I stammered, opening my eyes. "I — I'm not a pervert."

Jenner's gaze flicked my way, then back to her work. "You're dripping," she replied.

I gathered the towel tighter around my waist. "Uh, sorry."

Jenner motioned with her head. "The locker room's that-a-way."

"I know." I swallowed hard. "Somebody broke into my locker," I explained. "They stole everything."

"You still have your towel."

"Uh, yeah." I gave a nervous laugh. It didn't feel much like a towel anymore. More like a washcloth. A very tiny washcloth.

The projector hummed as it spun around. Jenner looked at me expectantly. I didn't know what to do, what to say.

"Would you like me to go to the main office for you?" Jenner asked finally. "I could get some clothes out of the Lost and Found."

My voice came out a whisper. "Yes. Please. Yes."

Jenner gave a quick nod. The film made a *flap-flap-flap* noise as it finished rewinding onto the reel. She flicked off the switch, put the film in its can, and pushed the projector toward the door. "Back in a flash," she said. A smile twitched at the up-turned corners of her mouth. "Sorry, that wasn't meant as a joke."

The door closed behind her.

"Well, *hello* there, Jenner." The Shark's voice. Even muffled through the door, it gave me the shivers. Quietly, I turned the lock, then plastered my ear against the door. "We're looking for somebody," The Shark went on, his voice as smooth and sweet as a Slurpee. "Have you seen a skinny kid, brown hair, wearing a towel? He's an escapee from the Sunny Brook Mental Home. We're very worried about him."

The Shark's cronies laughed. Ha-ha. Yeah, that Shark was a real wit.

Jenner laughed with them. "Yeah, I've seen him," she said.

My heart stopped.

"He went streaking across the playing field, about two minutes ago. The after-school girls' gymnastics club was chasing him."

Whew! *Saved.*

The Shark laughed. "Oh, man — this I gotta see." I heard running footsteps and the banging of the outside door. Then, after a long pause, the squeak of the projector's wheels receded down the hall.

Ten minutes later, there was a soft knock on the door.

"Who is it?" I asked, trying to disguise my voice.

"The Lost and Found. I've brought your delivery."

I unlocked the door and opened it a crack. A green eye stared back at me. It was the most beautiful eye in the world.

"Here." Jenner passed me a bulging, brown paper bag. "I hope this stuff fits. It's all I could find. Sorry about the socks." She closed the door before I had a chance to say thanks. I felt bad about that, because I knew after this moment, I could never, ever, *ever* face her again.

Inside the bag I found an old T-shirt, a pair of jeans that were three inches too short, one tennis shoe, one loafer, and a pair of pink socks with prancing unicorns. No underwear.

I dressed quickly, jammed my feet into the shoes,

then sneaked outside. I hid behind a pillar while I looked for The Shark. Coast was clear. I sprinted to the parking lot.

"Rob, where have you been?" Logan demanded when I reached his dad's car. "We've been waiting twenty-five minutes, sixty-three seconds."

I didn't say anything. Just slid in next to him on the seat.

"I even looked for you in the gym," Logan continued. "The Shark told me you'd already left, but I didn't think — hey, *wait* a sec." He peered over the top of his sunglasses, eyeing my socks. "What the — ?"

"Not one word," I interrupted. I held up a hand and sighed. "Please, not one single word."

The next day was Saturday. Most of my friends sleep in Saturday mornings, or veg-out on cartoons until lunch. Not Logan and me. That's our busiest pool-cleaning day. Usually, we can brush, vacuum, and check the chemicals of six pools, and still have time to go skateboarding by late afternoon.

Logan had been cleaning his family's pool for years. When we were in fifth grade, we started helping each other with our Saturday chores to get the work done faster, and eventually I became a pool-cleaning expert, too. In sixth grade, we decided to "pool our resources," as Logan joked, and go public. We printed information about our pool service on my computer, used our allowance for stamps, and mailed the flyers to just about every house in the neighborhood. Since most people around here have little kidney-shaped pools wedged into their backyards, business is always booming. We call ourselves Those Pool Guys.

"Who's first on our schedule today?" I asked Logan as we skateboarded to work.

Logan pulled a small notebook from his back pocket. He looked cool standing there all casual, hangin' five, reading his notes and pretending to be unaware that we were flying down the middle of a steep street. We both wore sunglasses and our THOSE POOL GUYS T-shirts.

"New customer today," Logan said, flipping his notebook shut. "Lady named Mrs. Thomas called. Lives over on Barker Pass. If she likes our work, she'll hire us full-time."

"Great."

Twenty minutes later, we arrived at Mrs. Thomas's house. It looked exactly like mine, except the floorplan was reversed. Instead of Pepto-Bismol Pink, it was painted Aim Toothpaste Blue.

A dark-haired woman with big gold earrings and green eyes answered the door.

"Good morning, ma'am," Logan said. He puffed out his chest and spoke in a you-are-a-valued-customer-so-I'm-going-to-sound-impressive voice. "We're Those Pool Guys. I believe you phoned me yesterday?"

She smiled. "Oh, yes. Hold on. Honey" — she called over her shoulder — "Those Pool Guys are here!"

"Which pool guys?" shouted a man's voice from the living room.

"Those Pool Guys."

"And I'm asking you *which* pool guys?"

Logan and I grinned at each other. We thought our name was pretty clever. Once people got the hang of it, they never forgot it.

"Dian," the man's voice called again, "*which* pool guys do you mean?"

Mrs. Thomas sighed and faced us with another smile. "Don't mind my husband. Hasn't had his morning coffee yet. Go around to the side gate, please. You'll find all the pool equipment in the little shed. If you have any questions, just knock on the back door."

"Will do, ma'am," Logan said. For a second, I thought he was going to salute.

We followed Mrs. Thomas's directions to the backyard. The pool was a typical kidney-shape, but everything else about the yard spelled *class*. The Thomases had a huge, glossy redwood deck with built-in seats and flower boxes. The patio furniture was bright white with rainbow-colored cushions and matching table umbrellas. They also had a changing room, outdoor shower, two rafts, diving board, *and* a slide.

We got to work right away. I netted leaves, while Logan checked the chlorine levels of the water. Hunched over the little tubes of chemicals, he looked like a mad scientist.

"Did you see the way she looked at me?" Logan asked a few minutes later.

"Who — Mrs. Thomas?"

"*No.* Gabriela."

"Gabriela? When?"

I must've sounded really confused, because Logan threw me an exasperated look. "Yesterday," he said, "in Wesley's class. Didn't you see her eyes? There was love in those eyes, Rob."

"I think," I said slowly, "those are contact lenses."

Logan shook his head. "Gabriela *wants* me, Rob. It's a Burning Desire."

"Maybe it's indigestion."

"No, it's love. I can tell."

"Logan, you're all wet," I said, laughing. I pulled the net on its long pole out of the pool and leaned it toward him. Water dripped onto his head.

"Hey!"

"Just trying to cool those burning desires," I said.

"Rob, quit it! I just moussed my hair!" Logan grabbed hold of the pole and jerked. I tumbled into the pool.

The Thomases didn't have a heater. My clothes sucked up the cold water like a sponge and suddenly weighed as much as a small iceberg. I sank straight to the bottom.

I'll get Logan for this, I thought. If *I'm* in, *he's* in.

I opened my eyes. They burned from the chlorine, but I could see a pair of tennis shoes and two legs rippling near the surface. With a fierce push, I shot into the air, my hand latching onto an ankle.

I took a quick breath and shouted, "Got you!"

"My mom is *not* paying you guys to mess around," said a girl's voice.

I looked up to see Jenner's black-green eyes staring down into mine. My hand jerked back as if her ankle had been a blowtorch.

If she remembers me, I thought, I'll have to drown myself.

"Hey, I know you," she said, peering closer. "Though I probably wouldn't have recognized you dry."

How did one go about drowning oneself? I wondered. Is there some special trick, or do you just open your mouth and swallow?

"I see you have clothes this time, but no towel," Jenner went on. Her mouth lifted in a half smile. "Would you like one?"

I opened my mouth to swallow and coughed on a gulp of water. Jenner must've taken that for a yes, because she hurried away.

I coughed and choked some more. Drowning was not the way to go. I started treading water.

"Here, man," Logan said, crouching down at the edge of the pool. "Give me your hand."

I glared at him. His lips were puckered like he was trying not to laugh.

"Rob, I'm sorry, buddy. I didn't mean to pull you in. Really. Truly. Now give me your hand."

"No," I said.

"Aren't you getting out?" he asked.

I shook my head. I planned to stay in the pool until Jenner graduated from high school and moved away.

She returned a few minutes later with a towel and her mom.

"Oh, you poor dear," Mrs. Thomas said. "You must be freezing. Climb out quickly, before you catch pneumonia."

The pneumonia part didn't sound too bad, especially if the disease became fatal before I reached the ladder. No such luck. I heaved myself out of the pool and squished over to where Mrs. Thomas had the towel waiting. My teeth started to chatter. I didn't look at Jenner.

"You'll need a hot shower, right away," Mrs. Thomas continued, steering me toward the house. "I'll put your clothes in the dryer. You can borrow a sweatsuit from my son. He's not home today and won't mind a bit. Your friend can finish the pool chores alone, can't he?" She threw a glance over her shoulder. Without waiting for Logan to answer, we went inside.

"I'm — I'm okay, really," I stammered as Mrs. Thomas led me down the hall. "I can go home like this. I don't mind."

She ignored me. "Here's the bathroom. The sweats are on the counter. You can pass your wet things to me through the door when you're ready."

I sighed, went into the bathroom, and kicked off my shoes. Getting the jeans off was harder. They were glued to my legs. I had to sit on the floor and peel them off.

I opened the door a ways and handed the dripping stuff to Mrs. Thomas.

"Thank you, dear," she said. "When you've finished your shower, Jenner will be glad to keep you company. Her room's right across the hall."

I gulped. No way, José. Somehow I'd have to sneak back out to the pool area and stay there till my clothes dried.

After a quick, hot shower, I hung my towel neatly on the rack, dressed in the bright red sweatsuit, and peeked out the door. The house was quiet, except for the faint *chug-chug* of a dishwasher running in the kitchen.

I tiptoed into the hall.

"Over here," Jenner called from her room. "Come on in."

Rats. Did the girl have supersonic ears?

I stepped into the doorway. Jenner sat at her desk, surrounded by film cans.

"I can't stay," I said. "I have to finish my pool work. Thanks anyway, though."

"Come back," Jenner insisted. "My brother will throw a triple fit if you get chlorine on his sweats, so you might as well stay and talk to me. Make yourself comfortable."

I inched into the bedroom. It wasn't anything like I expected. Winnie's room is pale blue and white with fluffy curtains and a canopy bed. She has lots of kids' books (of course) and about 246 stuffed animals. You couldn't tell the color of Jenner's room. The walls were completely covered with movie posters. Some were from old flicks like *Casablanca* and *Gone With the Wind*, but she had a few modern ones, too. The books in her bookcase were mostly about photography and filmmaking.

I perched on the edge of Jenner's bed.

"What's your name?" she asked.

"Rob."

"Rob what?"

"Rob Robin."

She smiled. "That's a funny name. Oh, sorry." She fingered one of her gold earrings. "I should know better. I get teased about my own name all the time. Jenner's the name of a town in northern California. My parents spent their honeymoon there. Pretty weird name for a kid, huh?" She shrugged. "But I like it."

"So do I," I agreed quickly. Maybe too quickly. I felt my cheeks get hot. To distract her, I said, "Uh, my real name is Christopher Robin."

"Your parents must like *Winnie-the-Pooh*."

"My mom does. Sometimes I think she married my dad just because of his last name."

Jenner laughed. It was a warm sound that made me feel relaxed inside, like drinking a hot mug of cocoa.

"My mom's bonkers on the subject of the Pooh stories," I went on. I sat further back on the bed and crossed my legs Indian-style. "My sister's name is Winnie, and we have a dog named Piglet and parakeets called Kango and Roo."

"Let me guess," Jenner said. "And a cat named Tigger?"

"No. In protest, I named him Steve."

Jenner grinned and her green eyes grew brighter. "You should be thankful your mom didn't name you Eeyore."

"You're right," I said and grinned back at her. Then I remembered she was an eighth-grader. I looked away.

"What classes do you have this semester?" Jenner asked.

"Math, English, art, American history." I paused for a breath. "Spanish, science, and P.E."

"Is that American history with Mr. Wesley?"

I nodded.

"I had that class last year," Jenner said, enthusiasm filling her voice. "Mr. Wesley is great. What are you doing for your oral presentation?"

I talked for several minutes, telling her about our idea for the time-travel news program.

"That sounds like fun, Rob. I wish my group had done something like that. I wonder . . ." She frowned slightly, tapping a pencil against her lips. "Hey, I know," she said, and jumped up. Sitting next to me on the bed, she cocked her head and smiled like she was going to share a secret. "How would you like to turn this news show of yours into something more realistic?"

"Sure. How?"

"Well, you could still be an anchorperson, reading news 'live' to the class, but you could interview the soldiers on videotape and run that part on a TV. It would look very professional."

I sat forward. "But where would we get a video camera?"

"The school has one," Jenner answered. "And guess who runs the A.V. department? Me. As long as I film on school property, there's no problem with me using the camera." She waved a hand at the film cans on her desk. "As you might have noticed, I like to make movies. When my grandpa died, I inherited his old super 8 movie camera. I've done a lot of films with it, but I'd really like more practice on a video. Plus, I could get some film credit for the photography club I'm in. What do you say, Rob?"

I couldn't talk. Our knees were touching in one tiny, little spot. And I could smell Jenner's hair. She smelled like summer and peaches.

"Rob — ?"

"Well, uh," I began, "I should really talk to the rest of my group first, but" — I inhaled more peaches — "but okay. The group's meeting at my house Monday, after school. Why don't you come by? We can all talk about it then."

"Great. Thanks, Rob." Jenner held out her hand.

I stared at it for a second, confused. Then I realized she wanted me to shake it. Her hand felt different from Winnie's. Bigger, of course. And with a firmer grip, though her skin was just as soft. Only Winnie's hand had never made my feet tingle.

Jenner squeezed my hand once more, then stood up. She said something about checking on my clothes, but I wasn't listening anymore. I sat there, looking down at my palm. The palm she had touched. The palm I would never, ever wash again.

TEN

On Monday after school, I raced into the house to get things ready for our group meeting. Since Jenner was joining us, I wanted everything to be better than perfect, and I only had an hour.

"Mom," I said, hurrying into the kitchen. "Mom, we have to talk. It's important."

She must have heard the tension in my voice. She looked up from her computer and frowned. "What is it, Rob?"

Gently, I tugged her elbow, leading her into the living room where we could get away from the screeching of Kanga and Roo. I scooped a pile of books off the couch. "Sit down, Mom. It's about the Heffalump."

She leapt to her feet. "What's happened to it? Did someone crash it? How could someone crash it? I've been here all day. Rob — "

"Nothing's wrong with the Heffalump," I said. (At least, nothing a few gallons of black paint couldn't fix.) "But I was hoping you could, you know, maybe move it into the garage. Just for the afternoon."

Mom propped her chin in her hands and looked me straight in the eye. "Your group is coming over today, and you're embarrassed by my true-blue, trusty van, is that it?"

I didn't answer.

Mom smiled and shook her head, her ponytail dancing. "No, I can't move the Heffalump into the garage. The garage is bursting at the seams. Your dad and I spent all morning stowing shipments of books out there."

She had to be kidding. There were still piles and piles of books and boxes all over the living room.

"Well, um," I began, "do you think you could park the Heffalump down the street? It would only be for a couple of hours."

"Of course. Sure. Why not?" She gestured at the door. "And maybe you'd like your dad and me to park ourselves out there, too?"

"Would you?" I asked hopefully.

"No."

"Well, okay. The Heffalump is good enough. Now, about these books . . ."

Mom's eyes narrowed. "Do you want *them* out on the street?"

"Actually, I was hoping for the garage, but maybe

we could just throw blankets over them or something."

"Honey, if you're ashamed about the way our house looks," Mom said with a funny smile, "why don't you just let your friends in through the bedroom window?"

I considered her suggestion for a moment, but decided Jenner might think it was too weird. And that was the whole point of this meeting with Mom: To "de-weird" our house.

"Okay, forget the books," I said. "I guess I'm really concerned about Dad. I'm afraid he's going to do something, well, something *strange*."

"Strange? Our family?" Mom touched her heart and looked shocked.

"Mom." My voice sounded desperate. "I just want to make sure Dad won't show my friends his appendix scar. Last year, at my birthday party, he told everybody he'd been attacked by a great white shark. I just hope he doesn't start showing off his stomach on Career Day."

Mr. Wesley had called Dad over the weekend. Everything was arranged. Two weeks from today, Dad would speak to the entire student body for twenty minutes about pro surfing. I planned to spend those twenty minutes in the boys' bathroom. I wasn't yet sure where I'd spend the rest of the school year.

Mom reached out and smoothed a strand of my hair. "Honey, what's up with you, hmm? You've had friends over lots of times. Why all the sudden worry and fuss?"

I shrugged and looked away. I couldn't tell her about Jenner. Especially since there wasn't anything to tell.

Yet.

Mom pulled a bouquet of keys from her sweatsuit pocket. "All right, Rob," she said softly. "I'll move the Heffalump."

"Thanks, Mom. Oh, wait. What about Winnie? Who — or what — is she today?"

Mom sighed. "Well, at school she became Sarah Cynthia Sylvia Stout Who Would Not Take the Garbage Out. Caused quite a, uh, stink. The teacher scheduled *another* parent conference with me for tomorrow." She sighed again. "But for the past few hours, Winnie's been reading quietly in her room."

"What's she reading?" I asked suspiciously. "*The Chainsaw Massacre?*"

Mom chuckled, heading for the door. "No, I think it's *King Bidgood's in the Bathtub*."

"Oh, no. I don't know that one. What's it about?"

"Calm down. It's a short, funny story about a king who decides to stay in the tub all day. He lunches there, fishes there, dances there, and no one can convince him to get out. It has a happy ending and everyone lives happily ever after. Nothing to worry about, Rob."

"You underestimate my sister," I replied, and tiptoed to her room. Peeking through the crack in Winnie's door, I could see her sitting on the carpet, her lips moving silently as she read. All 246 of her stuffed animals sat on the bed, arranged as if they were reading over her shoulder.

All calm — for now. I hoped things would remain that way.

Satisfied, I raced into my room to clean. I'd made my bed that morning, but now there was a lump in the middle. I whacked it. It bit me.

"Ouch! Sorry, Steve. Didn't know that was you." I smoothed the covers around him, shoved some loose papers into my desk drawer, and hung up a few clothes. By then I was feeling sweaty. Did I smell? I had showered after P.E., but I wanted to be extra clean for Jenner.

Next stop, the bathroom. I kicked off my shoes, then thrust an arm through the opening of the shower curtain to turn on the water.

Funny. I cocked my head, listening. Usually, the water made a shooshing sound in the tub. Today it went *splat-splatta-splat*.

I pushed open the shower curtain. There were books stacked in the tub. *Wet* books.

"Mom." I started hauling them out. Mom came up behind me and gasped.

"What are these doing in the shower?" I shouted.

"What are you doing taking a shower in the middle of the afternoon?" she shouted back. "There are a thousand dollars' worth of books in there, and you're ruining them!"

"I'm bailing as fast as I can!"

"Oh, for goodness' sakes, Rob, turn off the water!"

Oh, yeah. Hadn't thought of that.

Mom leaned over me and wrenched off the faucet. We stood there glaring at each other, breathing hard and dripping.

The doorbell rang.

The American history group had arrived.

The first part of the meeting went pretty well, all things considered. After Mom spread her soggy books out on the patio to dry, she served us a heaping plate of Dad's famous coconut macaroons and milk. Gabriela said nice things about my skateboard posters, and Jenner held Steve on her lap, petting him while he began a purring marathon. Logan didn't mention anything about Mom and me having wet hair. He was too busy watching Gabriela for any more signs of Burning Desire.

The best thing, though, was that The Shark hadn't come. He'd been absent from school that day, and I secretly hoped he'd contracted the bubonic plague over the weekend.

No such luck.

About halfway through our meeting, someone leaned on the doorbell.

I told the group to continue their discussion and went to answer the door.

The Shark stood there, hands in his pockets, whistling. He stopped long enough to say, "Hello, Weirdo."

I wanted to sock him in the nose. I wanted to tell him he was a creep, a jerk, a zit. I wanted to call the police and have him arrested for breaking into my locker. But I didn't have any proof. So instead I just said, "You're late."

He shrugged and pushed past me without waiting for an invitation.

"This way," I said coolly, and led him to my room. Nobody looked very glad to see him.

"Oooh, cookies and milk," The Shark sneered. "Just like kindergarten. Are we going to lie on our mats and have nappy time now?" He grabbed two handfuls of cookies and cruised over to my bed, flopping down on it. "Don't you guys have any beer?"

"Light or dark?" Logan asked. "Domestic or imported?"

The Shark wasn't listening. He'd noticed Jenner. "Hel-looo, baby," he said.

"Hello, sweetie-face," she replied, with a bored look.

The Shark glared at her.

Jenner smiled at me.

Logan rolled his eyes.

I mentally cheered.

"Could we get back to work, please?" Gabriela asked. She explained to The Shark about Jenner filming us, then read the notes she'd made on our discussion of the news script.

As she talked, I thought I heard someone running water again in the bathtub. Then I heard banging and clanging noises coming from Mom and Dad's closet. And *then* I heard what sounded like a dead body being dragged down the hall.

Jenner glanced at me. Logan wiggled his eyebrows, as if to say: *What's going on?*

I shook my head slightly. What *was* going on? What was Mom doing?

" . . . so now I think we should pick which people we'd like to play," Gabriela was saying. "Each one of us can research our characters, then we'll get together to start writing the script. Which character do you want to be, Mike?"

The Shark didn't answer. He was lying flat on his back, arms crossed behind his head, staring at the ceiling.

"Mike," Gabriela said, "are you listening?"

He shrugged.

"Look, remember what Mr. Wesley told us." She pointed a finger at him. "We all have to commit one hundred percent. If one of us doesn't partici- pate on this project, the whole group gets an F."

"Then you'll just have to do my research for me, won't you," The Shark said.

Now I heard laughing noises. And splashing noises.

Not Mom.

Winnie.

Gabriela threw up her hands. "Forget it, Mike!"

The Shark's voice came out smooth and sly. "It's better than getting an F, isn't it?"

Singing. Now Winnie was singing. Laughing, splashing, and singing. Piglet chimed in with a long, wavering howl. Kanga and Roo screeched. Steve leapt off Jenner's lap and dived under the bed.

Everyone stared at me. Jenner's eyes were wide.

"What kind of weirdos do you keep locked up in this looney bin?" The Shark asked. I could barely hear him over the ruckus.

"Back in a second," I mumbled and slipped out of the room.

The singing, screeching, and howling grew louder. I knocked on the bathroom door. "Winnie?"

Winnie sang: " *'Come in,' cried the King, with a trout, trout, trout. 'Today we fish in the tub!'* "

"What the — ?" I pushed open the door.

Winnie and Piglet sat in the middle of a frothing bubble bath. Kanga and Roo fluttered in a frenzy above their heads. The floor was flooded with water. Winnie wore Dad's rubber fishing waders, a crown made of aluminum foil, and was holding a fishing rod. Surrounding her were 246 soggy stuffed animals.

I slumped against the door. "Oh, Winnie . . ."

Piglet snapped at a bubble and sneezed.

"What do we have here?" said The Shark behind me. He peered over my shoulder.

Winnie gave a jolly laugh. " *'King Bidgood's in the bathtub, and he won't get out! Oh, who knows what to do?'* "

"Wait till I tell the guys at school about *this*!" The Shark chortled. "Come on, what are you waiting for, Christopher Robin. Aren't you going to get into the tub, too? The Midget Genius and the Seventh-Grade Weirdo Go Fishing!" He convulsed at his own humor.

"Is everything okay, Rob?" Jenner asked.

She and Gabriela and Logan had crowded through the door. They all stared at Winnie. Winnie waved.

Kanga circled the bathroom, then flew toward us, landing on top of Jenner's head.

Gabriela started to giggle. Then Logan. Even Jenner. The Shark was still laughing so hard, he could barely speak. "Wait'll I — tell — the guys — at school — " he repeated. "Wait'll I — tell — "

I couldn't stand it. I felt like I was going to explode.

"Get out!" I shouted. I shoved them all into the hall. Kanga squawked and flapped off Jenner's head. "Go on, get out! Go home!"

Jenner stopped giggling. Her mouth rounded into a perfect O.

"I said, get out! I don't want you here." I looked directly at Jenner. "*Any* of you!" I slammed the bathroom door in their faces. Then I whirled on Winnie.

"And *you*! I'm sick of your stupid little storybook game! That's right. That's all it is. A game. And it's ruining my life. When are you going to grow up? When are you going to stop being other people and start being *yourself*?"

I plunged my hand into the tub and pulled the plug. The water gurgled down the drain. Winnie and Piglet didn't say anything. They both stared at me, blinking.

I turned, almost slipping on the wet floor, and stomped out of the bathroom. Logan, Gabriela, Jenner, and The Shark were still standing there. I pushed past them without saying a word and slammed my bedroom door so hard that pictures rattled on the walls.

ELEVEN

I stayed in my room the rest of the afternoon and all that evening. Didn't even come out for dinner. Steve sat on my lap and purred while I stroked him, at least until he heard the can opener. Then he streaked to the door and meowed to get out. Traitor.

After dinner, both Mom and Dad asked if they could come in and talk to me. I told them (nicely) to go away. I didn't want to see or hear or talk to anyone in my family — especially Winnie. I was tired of Winnie messing up my life, of embarrassing me in front of my friends. *And* my enemies.

Logan phoned eight times. I refused each call. The last time he called, he disguised his voice and told Dad he was from Bill's Bike and Skate and that my bike was ready. What an insult to my intelligence! I never would've believed that ploy in a million years.

Later, Jenner called, too. I told Dad to say I was out of town on business.

"Are you sure you don't want to talk to her?" Dad asked through the door. "She seems upset."

"I'm sure," I answered. I didn't ever want to talk to Jenner again. I had loved her, and look what happened. She had laughed at me! Logan was right. I should've known better than to get mixed up with an eighth-grader.

The next morning, Mom knocked on my door.

"Rob, why aren't you up yet?" she called softly. "You'll be late for school."

I spoke into my pillow so that my voice sounded weak and muffled. "I'm not going. I'm sick."

Mom came into the room and put a hand on my forehead. "You don't feel hot."

I opened one eye and moaned.

"All right, all right," Mom said. "I'll take your temperature."

She left for a moment, then came back and slipped the thermometer into my mouth. When she left again to get Winnie out of bed, I held the thermometer against the light bulb of my lamp, the way I saw Elliot do in *E.T.*

Footsteps.

I jammed the thermometer under my tongue, burning it. Mom came back and peered at the little numbers. "Hmmmm," she said.

I rolled over and said feebly, "What does 'hmmmm' mean?"

"It means you're very ill."

"See? I told you."

"Yes. You have a temperature of one hundred and twenty-four."

"Oops."

Mom glared at me. "Yes. 'Ooops' is right. Now do you want to tell me what's *really* going on?"

"I don't feel good," I said. "Honest." It was true. When you know that everybody at school is going to laugh their heads off at you, you can't help but feel sick.

Mom sat on the edge of my bed. "Honey, what exactly happened between you and Winnie yesterday?"

I closed my eyes and turned my face against my pillow. "Why don't you ask *her*?"

"I did. She just blinked at me, the way she used to before she started talking. I hope she's not having a setback. She didn't eat any dinner, and she spent the entire evening sitting in her room, staring at her Monopoly game."

No weirder than usual, I thought.

"Rob?"

I didn't answer. I breathed real slow and deep, so Mom would think I was sleeping.

"All right, honey," she whispered. "Get some rest. We'll talk later."

After school, Logan barged into my room, plucked a dirty sock off the floor, and held it across his nose and mouth. "Are you contagious?" he asked.

"Yes," I said. "Go away."

He tossed the sock aside, then peered at me over the top of his sunglasses. He was wearing a black T-shirt with a picture of a blue MX missile on the front. The caption read: *When you care enough to send the very best.*

"You don't *look* sick," he said.

"Well, I am. Sick of you."

Logan clutched his chest, his face a grimace, and keeled backward onto my bed. "I'm wounded, Rob," he panted. "I'm hurt. I'm dying. Truly."

"You're squashing my feet," I said. "Get off me."

He scrunched around. "The Shark told practically everybody at school about yesterday."

"Who cares?" I pulled the covers over my head.

"*You* should. You gotta come back to school and defend your honor."

"Forget it, Logan. My honor's gone. Dead. Kaput. Wipe-out. Game over, man."

"Rob, this is *war*. You can't let The Shark win."

I threw back the covers. "He's already won. Besides, I thought I was supposed to act like a wimp. Let The Shark get bored with me. Well, that's what I'm gonna do. I'm staying in this bed until The Shark goes to high school, even if that takes six years."

"Rob, you can't."

"Oh, yes I can. It's the only way. Solves my problem with Career Day, too. Man, I can just imagine what The Shark will say when he sees Dad up on-stage." I shuddered.

"Rob — "

"Forget it. I'm never setting foot on the school grounds again."

"You have to," Logan said. Then he pulled a white envelope from his pocket.

"What's that?" I asked suspiciously.

He grinned. "A letter. A letter from Jenner. A letter from Jenner to *you*."

I started to grab it, then stopped. I folded my arms across my chest and sat back. "Take it away. I won't read it."

"Okay by me." Logan tossed the envelope on my lap, scooped up the apple Mom had left on my desk for lunch, and took a big juicy bite. "See ya 'round, Rob," he said. *Munch, munch.* "Get well soon, and all that rot." *Munch. "Hasta la zucchini."* He waved the apple and disappeared out the door.

I sat there, staring at the envelope. It was the first letter I'd ever gotten from a girl — if you didn't count my grandmother.

Jenner had written my name on the front in sharp, neat letters. There was no smiley face in the O like some girls do. She probably didn't dot her i's with hearts, either.

I picked up the envelope, intending to throw it away. Instead, I sniffed it. It didn't smell like Jenner at all. It smelled like a plain envelope. Like old glue.

My heart gave a funny squeeze. I couldn't stand it. I was furious with Jenner, and yet I couldn't stand it. I had to open that letter.

I ripped the flap. Inside was a piece of binder paper. The letter said:

Rob,
Meet me in the gym conference
room today at four o'clock. Pink
socks optional.

                              Jenner

I glanced at the bedside clock. Three-thirty. I doubted if Mom or Dad would drive me to school since I was supposed to be sick. And if I rode my skateboard, I'd never make it in time. Well, I'd just have to try.

I tore off my pajamas, threw on some clothes, grabbed my skateboard, and sneaked out of the house. Logan stood in the driveway, grinning at me.

"Here," he said, pointing to his BMX. "I thought you'd want to borrow this."

I made it to school with a minute to spare.

Jenner was waiting for me. She sat on the conference room table, swinging her legs real cool and casual. She wore a short jeans skirt and a big sweater the same color as an avocado. The color looked nice against her tan skin and made her smile shine extra-white.

"Hi," she said. "I see you decided to leave your pink socks at home."

I had to smile back. "Uh, yeah. I think I'll give them to my sister."

"That's who I wanted to talk about," Jenner said.

My insides tensed. It felt so good to see Jenner, that for a few seconds I'd forgotten about yesterday.

"Since you wouldn't talk to me on the phone last

night," Jenner continued, "I had to take drastic measures. I wouldn't have blamed you if you didn't show up. But Logan swore you would."

I could feel my face turning red. Sometimes, Logan knew me better than I knew myself.

"I wanted to apologize," Jenner went on. Her legs stopped swinging. "I know you're mad at me, and I'm really sorry. I didn't mean to hurt your feelings. And I didn't mean to laugh. It's just that your sister looked so cute in the bathtub, with all those stuffed animals and the dog, and then the bird landing on my head . . ." She stifled a giggle. "I wasn't laughing at *you*, Rob. I'm really sorry," she repeated.

I jammed my hands into my pockets and stared at the floor. "It's okay," I said.

"Thanks. I hope you aren't mad at me anymore."

I looked into Jenner's eyes. It sounds funny, but I felt like they were these two beautiful, polished pebbles, and I was the pond they'd been thrown into. I could feel little waves rippling inside me.

"No," I said, and my voice came out a croak. "I'm not mad." At least, I wasn't mad at her. Just Winnie.

Jenner smiled. "Hey, before I forget. The presentation group is going to meet at my house Saturday morning. After lunch, my mom said she'd drive us to the theater. There's a *Star Trek* movie marathon going on. Do you think you can come?"

"Yeah, sure! I'd like that." Then I felt like a set of sharp teeth had sunk into my ankle. "Uh, what about The Shark?" I asked. "I mean Mike. Is he coming, too?"

"Well, since he's in the group, we had to invite him to the meeting," Jenner said, "but I'll bet he doesn't show. What's with you guys, anyway? He and those two goons he hangs around with were making fun of you all day. I know The Shark doesn't really like anybody, but why does he hate you so much?"

I shrugged."I don't know. He's never said. Guess he's a shark of few words."

Jenner laughed. It was the kind of laugh I could listen to all day.

The door swung open. A janitor came in with a bucket and mop. "Hey, kids, school's closin' up now. Better get home."

Jenner and I walked outside together.

"Thanks for coming," she said. "See you Saturday."

My heart gave another funny squeeze. "Yeah," I answered. "See you Saturday." I hopped on Logan's bike and pedaled about eighty miles an hour all the way home.

TWELVE

When Mom discovered I'd sneaked out of the house to see Jenner, she gave me an ultimatum: "Either tell me what's going on between you and Winnie," she commanded, "or you're going back to school tomorrow. Uh-uh. No buts. No arguments. I don't care if you have a fever of a hundred and fifty-six. Now what's it going to be? Confession . . . or school?"

I chose school.

Big mistake.

On Wednesday, no matter where I was — in class, the cafeteria, hallways, even the bathroom — people around me would start singing the "Rubber Ducky" song.

On Thursday, when I went into Wesley's class, a giant box waited for me on my desk. A note taped to the box read: *For the Seventh-Grade Weirdo, From a Secret Admirer.* The box was filled with bars of deodorant soap.

On Friday, I got hit with a triple whammy. First, there was an editorial in our school newspaper that said "girls and boys should start showering together during P.E. in order to save water." The editorial was "signed" by me!

Then, sometime between third and fourth period, somebody poured eight boxes of bubble bath into the school swimming pool. A note attached to the diving board read: *Compliments of the Seventh-Grade Weirdo.*

And finally, during gym class, my locker was broken into again. This time, the thief not only stole my clothes, he left me a present: a giant, inflated yellow rubber duck.

"I can't take this anymore," I said to Logan after school. We sat on the parking lot curb, waiting for his dad. I was wearing more bizarre clothes from the Lost and Found, including a girls' T-shirt with the slogan: CALL ME, I'M AVAILABLE.

"I had such great plans for being invisible this year," I went on. "And now, because of Winnie and The Shark, everybody not only knows my name, they think I'm the weirdest weirdo alive."

"Rob, that's okay by me," Logan said, sounding like he was doing me the world's biggest favor. He draped his arm across my shoulders. "Yep. No doubt about it. Having a best friend like you is worth all the torture and embarrassment I've suffered."

"That *you've* suffered!" Just then, a group of gig-

gling girls passed us humming "Rubber Ducky."
"That *you've* suffered?" I repeated. "That's probably the two-thousandth time I've heard that song
this week. And I didn't see *you* sitting in the principal's office today, trying to plead your innocence
about editorials and . . . and bubble bath!"

"Remember the List, Rob. Just grit your teeth,
keep cool, and wimp out. The worst is over.
Probably."

"Yeah. I can hardly wait to see what The Shark
dreams up after my dad makes a fool of himself
and me on Career Day."

Logan wasn't listening. He suddenly started jerk-
ing his arms around like a robot gone haywire.
"Warn-ing, warn-ing, dan-ger, dan-ger," he said in
a nasal monotone. "Shark attack at twelve o'clock.
We repeat, shark attack at twelve o'clock."

I looked up. The Shark was cruising his bike
directly toward us. No time to run. He pulled a
wheelie, then skidded to a stop, spraying gravel at
our feet.

"Did you have a nice week?" he asked with his
iceberg smile.

"Yes, thanks. Very nice," Logan answered. "The
weather could've been a tad better, but — "

"Shut up," The Shark told him. "I was talking to
the Weirdo. Had enough, Christopher Robin?"

My hands clenched into fists. "Why don't you
leave me alone?"

"I was thinking of doing just that," The Shark
said. "I came to offer you a deal."

"What kind of deal?"

The Shark picked an imaginary piece of lint off

his shirt. "A deal you can't refuse, Weirdo. Here it is. I promise to make sure you don't get robbed anymore. Or teased. Or sent to the principal's office. We'll be buddies. Pals. Comrades."

"And what do I have to do?"

"Very simple," The Shark replied. "First, you see that I get to be anchorman for our history project. Then, you do all my research. And then you write my script. The day of the presentation, I'll stroll in, read the script, blow the doors off Wesley, and finally pass his class. I'll get an A, our group will get an A, and you'll never be bothered by me again."

Slowly, I stood up and faced him. "And what if I say no?"

"If you're smart, you won't," The Shark answered. "What's happened to you in the last two weeks is *nothing* compared to what will happen if you say no. Think about it. Let your imagination run wild. I'll expect your answer on Monday." He started to pedal away. "Have a nice weekend!"

After he'd gone, Logan gave a long, low whistle. "Man, what are you gonna do?"

"I don't know." I thought about The Shark's offer. Had to admit, it was tempting. If I did what he asked, there'd be no more Seventh-Grade Weirdo. I could be a normal guy again, just like everyone else. That's what I'd always wanted. And yet . . .

I sighed. "Logan," I said, "I really don't know."

The second I got home, I knew something was wrong. That's because the house was *quiet*.

I crept cautiously through the kitchen and peeked into the living room. Five pairs of eyes swiveled toward me. Mom, Dad, Winnie, Piglet, and Steve were all crammed together on one couch, waiting. Waiting for me, though Piglet was the only one who looked glad to see me. He leapt to his feet and started panting happily. Mom turned and gave him a warning look. He collapsed again with his head on his paws, his eyes wide and guilty.

"Where have you been?" Mom asked, not even fazed by my weird outfit. She stood up and crossed her arms. "You're late."

"I had Logan's dad drop me off at Bill's Bike and Skate. I wanted to see if my bike was ready."

"And is it?"

"No."

"Fine. Sit down."

Dad got up and motioned for me to take his place next to Winnie. She and I stared at each other for a second, but didn't say anything.

"What's going on?" I asked, not really sure I wanted to know.

"Your mother and I are concerned," Dad replied. "I know that we're all very busy with our own private lives, but for the last few days, this family has not been much of a family."

Mom nodded. "There's something wrong between you and Winnie, and I'd like to know what it is."

I glanced at my sister, who just blinked at me. "There's nothing wrong," I answered. I busied myself scratching Steve behind the ears so no one could see my face.

Mom made a noise like a snort. Piglet sneezed in reply.

"Listen," said Dad, "just because we're parents doesn't mean we're stupid. Something's up and I'd stake my quiver of surfboards on it. You and Winnie haven't said two words to each other in four days."

"Actually," Mom put in, "Winnie, you haven't said one word to *anyone* all week. All you've done is sit in your room after school, cutting little pieces of paper, and gluing them onto that perfectly good Monopoly game.

"And as for you," she continued, pointing a finger at me, "you've spent the same amount of time sitting around in *your* room, doing heaven knows what."

She made it sound as if I were concocting plans to blow up the world. All I'd been doing was writing Jenner's name about six hundred times in my notebook and thinking about her green eyes.

"Well?" Dad asked.

"Well?" Mom repeated.

I swallowed. "Well, what?"

Dad threw up his hands. "Cowabunga, Rob! We want to know what's been going on, and we want to know *now*."

Winnie and I glanced at each other again. Her eyes were as big and sad and guilty as Piglet's. My heart grew warm for a second, like it does when I drink chicken noodle soup, and I had a sudden urge to reach over and hold her hand. But then I remembered how she'd embarrassed me this week, and practically every single week since she'd been born.

The warm feeling disappeared. I felt like I'd swallowed an ice cube.

"I have nothing to say," I told Dad. My voice sounded hollow.

Mom looked at Winnie. "How 'bout you, Pooh?"

Winnie gazed at Mom and blinked. Then she answered in a quiet voice I didn't recognize. "I have nothing to say, too. Everything's fine with Rob and me."

"Aaarrrgggh!" Mom said in frustration, her ponytail switching. She turned on Dad. "I *told* you we should've tried the Attila the Hun approach. Anything would be better than tiptoeing around like Sugar Plum Fairies."

"Nina, we can't force them to talk if they don't want to talk!"

"Yes, I know, but we can't let this go on!"

"Well, what do you suggest? Feeding them stale bread and gruel? Chaining them in the basement?"

"We don't have a basement," said Winnie.

"You keep out of this!" Mom cried.

Kanga and Roo started screeching, as if imitating Mom and Dad. Then with a yelp, Piglet leapt to his feet and ran from the room, his tail between his legs. Piglet hates to hear people shout.

"May I please be excused?" Winnie interrupted softly.

Mom slumped into a chair. "Yes, yes, go. I'm sorry I yelled. I'm feeling very frustrated with you children right now, so *both* of you can go to your rooms. And I want you to sit in there until dinner and think about what's wrong between you."

"Yes, Mom," Winnie said.

I followed her down the hall. As she scurried through her door, I caught a glimpse of her room.

The floor was carpeted with scraps of colored paper, glue and scissors, and other odds and ends. I wondered what she was making.

Alone in my room, I tried not to think about The Shark and the deal he'd offered me. Instead, I thought about Jenner. In nineteen hours, twelve minutes, forty-two seconds, I'd be sitting next to her at the movie theater. We'd laugh together at Mr. Spock, and I'd buy a popcorn for us to share, and maybe we'd reach into the box at the same time and our hands would touch and then . . .

And then, something clicked in my mind. Something about Winnie.

A few moments ago, in the living room, Winnie had said five complete sentences. Five! And all of them in a normal voice. Not in Mrs. Frisby's or Bilbo Baggins's or King Bidgood's, but in a voice I hadn't recognized because I'd never heard it before. None of us had ever heard it before.

Winnie had spoken in her *own* voice.

What was going on?

THIRTEEN

At last it was the day. Saturday. Jenner Day.

I got up extra early, took an extra long shower, and chose my clothes with extra care. I even patted a bit of Dad's cologne on my cheeks and neck.

"What's that smell?" Logan said when I met him at his house.

I shrugged. "What smell?"

He snuffled like an anteater, then wrinkled his nose. "Ewww, is Mrs. Rehler fertilizing her lawn again? No, no, wait a minute." *Sniff, sniff.* "Rob, it's coming from you!"

"Do I smell that bad?" I asked, taking a step backward.

"Well, you won't after I hose you down."

"Oh, no!" I flipped directions on my skateboard

and started for home. I'd have to take another shower.

"Rob, wait!" Logan called after me. "Where are you going? I was just kidding! You smell nice. Rob, stop!"

I stopped. "Does that mean I usually *don't* smell nice?"

"No. You smell okay, I guess. I'm not an expert, you know. I don't usually go around smelling guys. Come on." We turned back, heading toward Jenner's house. "So tell me," Logan continued. "How do you like my new T-shirt? I got it especially for my first date with Gabriela."

He puffed out his chest. His shirt read: SO MANY GIRLS, SO LITTLE TIME.

I sighed and shook my head. "I don't know, Logan. . . ."

"Trust me," he said. "Gabriela will swoon when she sees I've chosen her out of thousands."

"Uh-huh."

We zoomed down the hill, the houses along the street looking like a blur. It felt kind of nice, having a free Saturday. Logan had rescheduled all our pool-cleaning jobs for the next day.

"Hello, boys," Mrs. Thomas said when she opened the door.

"Who's there?" Mr. Thomas called from the living room.

"It's just Those Pool Guys, dear."

"*What* pool guys?"

Mrs. Thomas sighed with a smile. "I don't want to go through *that* again, do you, boys? Come on in. Jenner and Gabriela are waiting for you in the family room. It's the door at the end of the hall."

"Hi, Rob. Hi, Logan," Gabriela greeted us. "You're right on time." She opened her notebook on the coffee table, her pencil poised and ready for notetaking.

Jenner sat next to her on the loveseat. She was wearing the *Star Trek* sweatshirt again, and had her hair tucked behind her ears. She gave a little wave. My heart felt like a basketball player was dribbling it at tornado speed. I just stood there and stared into her beautiful green eyes. I must've stood there for a long time.

"Ahem, ahem, ahem." Logan cleared his throat, sounding like he was going to toss a furball. I jumped, startled. "Sorry," he said, "must've had an obstruction in my esophagus. Don't worry. I'm okay now. You won't have to perform the Heimlich Maneuver or anything."

Gabriela looked relieved. Logan must've thought her relief was True Love, because he hurried over to the loveseat and wedged himself between her and Jenner. Gabriela tried to scoot as far from him as possible, which was about half an inch. I sat on the floor.

"Has anyone heard from Mike?" Gabriela asked, looking at her watch. "We need to get started if we're going to make the movie by noon."

"Uh, I don't think he's coming," I said.

"Why not?"

"Well — " I stopped. I wasn't sure I wanted anyone else to know about The Shark's deal. At least, until I knew what to do about it.

Logan pushed his sunglasses up onto his head.

"Gabriela has a right to know, Rob," he advised. He sounded like I was about to inform Gabriela that she had only two days to live. "After all, she *is* our chairperson."

"I know, I know."

"What's going on, Rob?" Gabriela asked.

I took a deep breath — then told her and Jenner about The Shark's threats and demands.

"But . . . but that's blackmail!" Gabriela cried. "Or is it extortion? I always get those two confused. And besides, I wanted to be the newscaster."

"What are you going to do, Rob?" Jenner asked.

I thought back to Reed's *Secrets to Surviving Seventh Grade*. If I wimped out, as his list advised, things would quiet down and I'd be safe again. But if The Shark knew he could blackmail me once, what was to stop him from doing it again?

"I think you should tell Mr. Wesley," Jenner said, interrupting my thoughts. "He'll know what to do. It's not fair for you guys to get graded down just because you're stuck with someone like The Shark. What do you think, Logan?"

"Hmmmm. What do *you* think, Gabriela?"

"I agree with Jenner."

"Then I do, too," Logan said quickly.

"And," continued Gabriela, "I think all of us should talk to Mr. Wesley together. Monday before class. Agreed?"

I nodded, though I wasn't so sure Mr. Wesley could help. I mean, he could transfer The Shark out of our group or something, but how could he stop The Shark from making my life miserable forever?

"Okay, that's settled," Gabriela announced.

"Let's get to work. Rob, have you decided what character you want to play?"

I opened my bookpack, pulling out a binder. "Yeah. I want to be Patrick Henry."

"Okay. Let's pretend I'm the newscaster, and I'm interviewing you." Gabriela picked up a microphone from an old tape recorder. She held it in front of my face and said, "Good morning, Mr. Henry. I have a few questions I'd like answered for our viewers. Tell me, don't you think all this war talk is silly? Don't you think we should try to get along with the British to keep things peaceful?"

I thought for a minute, then riffled through my notes. I'd copied down a quote from Henry that was perfect for Gabriela's question.

I cleared my throat, sat up straight, and spoke into the microphone. My voice boomed. " 'Is life so dear, or peace so sweet, as to be purchased at the price of chains and slavery? Forbid it, Almighty God! I know not what course others may take; but as for me, give me liberty, or give me death!' "

Silence.

Jenner stared at me. Gabriela stared at me. Logan stared at me as if I'd turned into a lunatic.

Then, softly, Jenner started clapping.

I realized that sometime during my little speech, I had stood up, my fist raised at an unseen enemy.

"Uh, sorry." I lowered my arm and sank back onto the floor.

"Why are you apologizing?" Jenner asked. "That was great, Rob. Really great. You sounded so . . . so *real*. Wow, look at my arms — goose bumps!"

I didn't know what to say. "Thank you," I finally answered. "You know a lot about movies and acting and stuff. So . . . thanks."

Gabriela was nodding. "Let's use that in the script, Rob. That was really good." She made a few notes in her book. "Okay, Logan. What character are you going to play?"

Logan yawned and gave a luxurious stretch, his arm coming down across Gabriela's shoulders. "I had my heart set on Paul Revere's horse," he began. "I mean, has anyone ever tried to understand the *animal's* point of view . . . ?"

Gabriela rolled her eyes. I ignored her and Logan, and glanced at Jenner. She was still rubbing the goose bumps on her arms. When she caught me watching her, she smiled. A different smile. A special smile. A smile meant only for me . . .

We worked all morning and got several pages of our script written. At eleven, Mrs. Thomas served us fruit and sandwiches for lunch, then drove us to the movies.

I don't think Logan had a very good time. Gabriela grabbed an aisle seat, and pulled Jenner into the seat next to her. Quickly, I sat beside Jenner. Logan informed the theater at large that at social events the proper seating arrangement is boy-girl-boy-girl, but Jenner and Gabriela wouldn't budge. Heaving a huge sigh, Logan finally slumped into the seat next to me. He spent the next hour running back and forth to the concession stand about fifty times, trying to bribe Gabriela with popcorn and sodas and candy bars. Nothing worked. So Logan went to sleep.

Jenner and I shared a large popcorn. Although our hands never accidentally touched, I had a great time anyway. Actually, I had more fun watching Jenner than I did watching the films. Jenner didn't act like some girls. You know, the kind that are always fussing with their hair and giggling and stuff. Instead, she cheered and clapped and whistled during the exciting parts, just like I did. And in one scene, where Mr. Spock dies, she must have seen me wipe my eyes.

"It's okay, Rob," she whispered, squeezing my arm. "He comes back alive in the next movie." I nodded, and noticed her green eyes glistened.

Mr. Thomas picked us up at six o'clock. He dropped me off at home first.

"That was fun," Jenner said as I opened the car door.

"Yeah, fun," mumbled Logan with a scowl.

"Let's do it again soon," Jenner continued.

"Only at gunpoint," Logan muttered.

I elbowed him in the ribs. "Okay, soon," I said to Jenner and slammed the door. She waved, and the car backed out of the drive.

She wanted to see me again!

Jenner.

An eighth-grader.

Wanted to see *me*.

I practically cartwheeled into the house.

Mom and Dad met me at the door.

"Hello, hello!" I sang. "How are you? What's for dinner? Isn't it a *great* day?"

"Is Winnie with you?" Mom asked urgently. Her eyes looked red, and I noticed her ponytail was crooked.

"No," I said, "but I could have her beamed up."

"This is no time for jokes." Mom grabbed my arm so hard, it hurt. "Have you seen Winnie at all today? Did you see her this morning? Did she go to Jenner's with you?"

I shook my head.

"Oh, *no*." Mom began to pace.

Dad put an arm around her and steered her into the living room. "It's all right, Nina," he soothed. "Just sit down for a minute, and we'll think this through. It's all right."

My stomach felt hollow. "What's wrong?" I asked. "Mom, what's wrong?"

Dad eased Mom into a chair, then looked at me. His face was pale beneath its tan. "It's Winnie — " he began. "She — she's missing."

FOURTEEN

I felt like Captain Kirk had shot me with a phaser gun. Kind of numb and weak. "Winnie's . . . missing?"

Mom nodded, rubbing her eyes. "When we got up for breakfast, she was already gone. We've looked all over the neighborhood. No one's seen her."

"Maybe she's at a friend's house," I suggested.

"You forget," Dad said, patting Mom's shoulder. "Winnie doesn't have any friends."

I stood silent for a moment. I thought about the bathtub incident on Monday. And not speaking to Winnie for a week. "Maybe she ran away from home," I said. "Did she take anything with her? A suitcase or something?"

"Her Monopoly game is missing," Dad replied.

I almost laughed. "Her Monopoly game? She took her *Monopoly* game?" Geez, leave it to my sister not to worry about food or shelter. Just boredom.

"John," Mom said, looking up into Dad's eyes, "we've waited long enough. We've got to call the police.

The police.

My insides felt cold. Horrible scenes flashed through my mind. Winnie trapped in some abandoned refrigerator. Winnie mauled by wild dogs. Winnie kidnapped . . .

The doorbell rang.

Dad hurried to answer it. A tall man with neatly combed silver hair, and wearing a gray, three-piece suit, stepped into the entryway. He held a Monopoly game in one hand and my sister in the other.

"Winnie!" Mom flew across the room. She gathered Winnie into her arms, and started crying and kissing and saying, "Oh, Winnie, oh, Winnie, oh, Winnie."

Dad reached out and gently touched the top of Winnie's head. "Thank you," he said, his voice soft. "Thank you for bringing our daughter home." Then he turned, pumping the man's hand. "Thank you so much. We've been frantic."

"I'm sure you have been," the man replied. "I apologize for not bringing her sooner. I had no idea she was out without permission or supervision."

Dad looked puzzled. "Where did you find her?"

"Well, I didn't exactly find her, Mr. Robin," the man said, chuckling. "She found *me*."

"I don't understand."

"May I sit down?" the man asked. "Then I'll explain everything."

Dad motioned toward a chair. I joined Dad on the couch.

"My name is Travis Young," the man said, handing Dad a business card. "I'm the president of Kid Stuff. You might have heard of us. We're the largest toy and game company on the West Coast."

"Yes, of course," Dad said. He looked at the card, then passed it to me.

"I've heard of you," I said, impressed. "I have some of your video games. They're great."

Mr. Young nodded with a smile. "Thank you. I'm in town this weekend representing my company at an international toy and game exhibition. Your daughter came by my booth today, out at the fairgrounds, and — "

"Winnie!" Mom exclaimed. She was still kneeling on the floor, with my sister in her arms. "Winnie, how on earth did you get to the fairgrounds?"

Winnie shrugged. "I took the bus."

"You *what*?!"

"Cowabunga, Winnie!" broke in Dad. "We've been worried *sick* about you! If you wanted to go to the fair, why didn't you just ask — "

"You took the bus by yourself?" Mom interrupted. "Winnie, you're only five years old! That's too young to ride the bus alone. Don't you understand that something bad could've happened — "

"Don't you ever, *ever* do something like this again!" Dad shouted.

"Never!" Mom agreed.

Piglet started to howl. Kanga and Roo started to screech. I put my hands over my ears. Winnie just blinked.

"Please!" Mr. Young said in a calm but firm voice. "Please, I'd like to tell you *why* Winnie came to see me today."

"This had better be good," Mom said, giving her ponytail a jerk. She sat next to me, my sister firmly pinned in her lap.

Mr. Young took Winnie's Monopoly game from its box and unfolded it onto the coffee table. Piglet came over and sniffed it.

"Your daughter has done something quite ingenious," Mr. Young said. "She's invented a prototype for a new board game, and she came to me hoping I'd like to manufacture it. And I want to. Most definitely."

I noticed that the Monopoly game didn't look like Monopoly anymore. Winnie had completely covered the board with colorful new squares and designs.

"Winnie, perhaps you'd like to explain the game to your parents," Mr. Young urged.

Winnie wiggled out from under Mom's grasp. "It's called Once Upon a Time," she began quietly. "It's kind of a combination of Trivial Pursuit and Pictionary and a couple of other games all rolled together. Each player gets to be a character from a famous children's book or story. You travel through enchanted lands and do daring deeds and answer riddles" — she pointed these sections out on the board — "but you have to stay in character. The object of the game is to live happily ever after. It takes a lot of work, and a lot of thinking, but it's fun."

Winnie smiled at me, then climbed back up onto Mom's lap.

Mom, Dad, and I didn't say anything. We just stared at Winnie with our mouths hanging open. I'm sure Mr. Young thought we were impressed with Winnie's game — and we were. But we were more impressed by the longest speech she had ever made *in her own voice*.

"Of course, the game needs a little work," Mr. Young said. "We'll have to develop the game board more thoroughly, and do a bit more research in the children's book field, but that shouldn't take long. I'd like to begin manufacturing this immediately. I think we can have at least one hundred thousand games made before Christmas."

Mr. Young pulled a small calculator from his pocket and tapped out some numbers. "With the game retailing at thirty-five dollars, we'll gross over three million in sales before the first of the year. And that's just the beginning. Of course, I'm prepared to make a generous offer for all rights to the game." He smiled at Winnie. "Mr. and Mrs. Robin, if this gamble works, your daughter will soon be a millionaire."

Winnie — a millionaire! My mind felt dizzy. She could retire at age six. She could buy eight thousand stuffed animals. Or have a limo and chauffeur drive her to school. She'd never need an allowance again.

"The fact that she's only five will be a plus with the advertising and publicity," Mr. Young continued. "That is, if you approve of her making the commercials. I'll guarantee that those will be properly supervised."

I started to feel that familiar fist in my stomach. Commercials. And publicity. That meant there'd soon be national newspaper articles about Winnie, and television interviews, and maybe even lecture tours. Winnie would be famous all over again. Everyone would know her name . . . and mine.

"I can tell I've overwhelmed you," Mr. Young said, looking at Mom and Dad with their mouths still hanging open. "Why don't you think about this tonight. Look over my company's brochure, and read carefully through these standard contracts." He pulled a thick bundle of papers from his suit pocket and laid them on the table. "Perhaps you'd give me a call, say, tomorrow morning? Then we can set up another meeting. I'm sure you'll have a number of questions."

"Yes. Yes, of course," Mom murmured.

Mr. Young slapped his hands on his knees, then stood up. He shook Dad's hand. "Thank you, Mr. and Mrs. Robin. Please call tomorrow, as soon as possible. Remember, time is of the essence." He smiled down again at my sister. "Good night, Winnie. See you later. I'll just let myself out." He closed the door quietly behind him.

Dad and Mom both let out a long sigh.

"Winnie," Dad said in wonder, "this is amazing. This is wonderful . . ."

Mom was chuckling, shaking her head. "Wherever did you get the idea to do this, sweetheart?" she asked.

"From Rob," Winnie answered.

"From *me*?"

Winnie cocked her head and blinked, like she couldn't understand why I was confused. "You got mad at me on Monday. You said I was playing a storybook game. You asked me when I was going to stop being other people and start being myself. So I *did*. Except, it was fun being other people. So I made a game where people could be anything they wanted to be. I did it for fun. And so you wouldn't be mad at me anymore."

The fist clenched tighter in my stomach. My throat ached. Part of me wanted to hug Winnie, but another part of me didn't ever want to see her again. I felt like blurting out, *But now you've made it worse!* But I didn't. I couldn't. . . .

I looked away from Winnie's sad, brown-bear eyes. "May I please be excused?" I asked Mom and Dad. "I — I think I need to rest for a while. All this excitement. And you probably have things to talk over."

Without waiting for an answer, I stumbled into my room. I collapsed onto my bed, burying my face into a pillow. Everyone in the world was going to know who Winnie was now. And they'd know who I was, too! Because I'd be the brother of the kid genius. The kid who invented the game. The kid who was a millionaire. Everyone would tease me, even worse than before. The Shark especially. I would never escape. This year I'd be the Seventh-Grade Weirdo. And next year, the Eighth-Grade

Weirdo. And then the Ninth. The Tenth. And so on and so on, until one day, hobbling around with a cane and tuning my hearing aid, I'd become the Grandfather Weirdo. And it was all Winnie's fault. . . .

FIFTEEN

Mom and Dad sat up practically all Saturday night discussing Winnie's game and contract. I know because I lay awake all night *listening* to them discuss Winnie's game and contract. The longer they talked, the longer I listened. The longer I listened, the harder that fist got in my stomach, until I felt as if I'd swallowed a chunk of sidewalk.

Finally, at three A.M., I got up and marched into the living room.

"Can you please keep it down?" I said, my voice coming out cross. "Some people in this house are trying to sleep, you know."

"Oh, sweetheart, I'm sorry," Mom said. "I didn't realize how loud we were talking."

She and Dad, wearing their pajamas, looked at

me with bleary eyes from where they sat on the floor. Piglet lay nearby. They were completely surrounded by papers.

"It's this contract," Dad said. "We're under attack, and it's closing in, fast. Now I know how Custer felt at his last stand."

Mom nodded, her hair coming loose from its ponytail. "Just look at page one, Rob. Wait a minute — where is page one? Piglet, get your chin off that paper! John, the darn dog has drooled all over the contract! This lawyer-talk is hard enough to read without dog drool smearing the ink!"

"Give it here." Dad dabbed at the page with the hem of his bathrobe, then handed it back to her.

"Look at page one, Rob," Mom repeated. "With all these 'heretofores' and 'hereinafters,' we can't make heads or tails of it. It *looks* like a good deal. It looks like Winnie will make a lot of money. But for all we know, to do it she may have to give up her firstborn child."

"Well," I said, trying to sound casual, "maybe signing a deal with Kid Stuff isn't such a good idea right now."

"What do you mean?" Dad asked.

"I mean, you shouldn't rush into anything. Take some time to think about the contract. Like, maybe, five or ten years."

"Five or ten years!" Mom exclaimed.

"Uh, you know, until Winnie matures enough to understand what's going on."

Dad laughed. "Don't worry about Winnie's maturity, Rob. At her rate, she'll probably have a law degree by fifth grade."

"Wait a minute," Mom said. "I think Rob has a point."

My hopes soared.

"Winnie may be a genius mentally," she continued, "but emotionally, she's still a five-year-old. How do we know she can cope with all the fame? What she's experienced so far because of reading abilities and impersonations is *nothing* compared to what will happen once this game hits the market. And look how hard it's been for her, fitting in with the other kids at school."

Dad frowned. "True."

"And then there's the money. A five-year-old doesn't have any concept of what it means to be a millionaire."

"Also true," Dad agreed.

Way to go, Mom, I cheered inside. Dad's teetering on the edge! Push him just a bit further. Then we can tear up the contract, forget the whole thing, and my life can get back to normal.

"Maybe we *are* rushing things," Dad said. "I think we should look into this further before we make a decision."

I nodded vigorously. "That's wise, Dad. Yes. Right. Absolutely."

Dad stood up, tightening the belt of his bathrobe. "First thing in the morning, let's call our lawyer. We'll have her come out immediately and go over the contract with us. If and only if she's stoked, we'll sign on the dotted line."

My hopes crashed like a lead zeppelin.

"And as for Winnie," Dad said, "well, she's got an awesome family to love and support her. We'll keep her from wiping out along the way, won't we, Rob?" He clapped an arm around my shoulder.

"Yeah, sure, Dad," I mumbled.

He beamed. "Radical! Now let's get some sleep."

Mom and Dad called their lawyer at nine the next morning. By ten, Ms. Baker was sitting in our living room, reading the contract, and making little hmmm-what-do-we-have-here noises in the back of her throat.

All of us clustered around her, including Piglet and Steve.

"Well?" said Mom.

"Well?" said Dad.

"Well," Ms. Baker said, adjusting her glasses. "If the Party hereto executes said Agreement, she will, of course, enter into said Agreement pursuant to and in accordance with the provisions set up by the manufacturers. You understand, these provisions will govern and protect the rights and liabilities of both Parties. Now, in consideration of the premises contained herein, the Parties hereto agree as follows . . ."

"What?" asked Mom.

"What?" asked Dad.

Ms. Baker sighed. "Let me put it another way. If the Party hereto executes said Agreement, then Kid Stuff shall have the sole and exclusive right to manufacture, sell, and distribute said product. However, the Party will be compensated with a considerable advance against royalties to be earned at the rates hereinafter set forth."

"What?" asked Mom.

"What?" asked Dad.

"She means," interrupted Winnie in her quiet voice, "that you should sign the contract. I'm going to be a millionaire."

"Yes," Ms. Baker agreed, looking at us over the top of her glasses. "That is, in essence, what I meant."

Dad laughed. "Well, why didn't you say so? Let's call Mr. Young, get him over here, and start the ball rolling!"

That ball turned into an avalanche.

Mr. Young got here so fast, I suspected he had a phone in his car and was parked at the end of the block. After answering a few questions, he, Mom, and Dad signed the contracts, Winnie got her first of several hefty checks, and Mr. Young called an immediate press conference. Photographers filled our house, taking pictures of Winnie and Mr. Young, toasting each other with champagne glasses filled with Kool-Aid. By the next morning, every major newspaper across the country knew about Winnie. And they all featured big, bold headlines and breathless articles about her road to riches that would begin with Once Upon a Time.

Two weeks before, Mom had told me that junior high students never read newspapers. *Wrong!* On Monday, kids in every single one of my classes were talking about Winnie. They pointed at me, and whispered, and giggled, saying, "That's him! He's the one! The Seventh-Grade Weirdo is her brother!"

The Shark knew, too.

"Hey, Weirdo," he began with his icy smile. He

and his two cronies were lounging in front of Wesley's door before class. "I forgot my lunch money today, Weirdo. Could you loan me a couple thousand?"

His cronies made *heh-heh-heh* sounds in their noses. I tried to ignore them and keep walking, but The Shark grabbed my arm.

"It's Monday," he sneered. "I hope you thought about my offer very carefully this weekend. The deadline for your decision is *now*."

I shook off his hand. "You'll get your answer in a few minutes," I said, trying to keep my voice cool. Then I strolled into the classroom.

Gabriela and Logan stood talking to Mr. Wesley. Even Jenner was there. I hurried to join them. Jenner gave me a wide smile, but I was so embarrassed about Winnie that I looked away.

"I hear you have something to discuss with me about your group," Mr. Wesley said.

"Yes, sir."

"I'm all ears, Rob."

I cleared my throat. "We're having some problem with The Shark — I mean, Mike Sharkey. He refuses to come to our group meetings. And when he does show up, he doesn't do any work."

"I see."

"Mr. Wesley, that's not even the half of it!" Jenner said indignantly. "Mike *threatened* Rob last Friday. He swore he'd do all sorts of horrible things to Rob if Rob doesn't do Mike's work for the presentation."

"Is this true?" Mr. Wesley asked, looking at me.

"It sure is," answered Logan. "I'm a witness. I was there. I heard *everything*."

"Rob?" Mr. Wesley prompted.

I was probably signing my death warrant, but I had to answer. It was the only way to deal with The Shark.

I nodded. "It's true, Mr. Wesley."

"All right. Thank you, Logan. Gabriela. And you, too, Jenner. Rob, I'd like to speak to you alone for a few minutes. Gabriela, when class starts, would you take roll, please? We'll be right back."

Mr. Wesley guided me out the door. The Shark's eyebrows lifted in surprise when he saw me with the teacher, and his hands clenched into fists. I knew he was watching us with those black, empty eyes as we made our way down the hall. And I wondered what evil thoughts were churning in his mind when he saw Mr. Wesley open the door to the principal's office.

"Why don't you tell me exactly what's been going on, Rob," said Mrs. Curtis, our principal, a few minutes later. She sat across from me at her desk, her hands clasped in front of her. She looked a lot more understanding today than she had last week, when I'd been called in about the newspaper editorial and the bubble-bath-in-the-swimming-pool incident.

Mr. Wesley gave my shoulder a gentle squeeze of encouragement. "Go on, Rob," he coaxed. "This time, Mrs. Curtis will believe you." He moved to leave, giving the principal a quick nod.

I took a deep breath. And then I started talking. The words spun out as fast as those rubber bands that twirl the propellers of a toy airplane.

When I finished explaining everything The Shark had done to me since school started, Mrs. Curtis sighed.

"Yours is not the first complaint I've received about Mike," she said. "In fact, this is the last straw. Not to make light of your predicament, Rob, but Mike is responsible for even worse things on this campus, and I think it's time to take serious action." She marked something down on a pad of paper. "Thank you for coming to see me. Oh, and would you send Mike in next, please?"

I returned to class. When I told The Shark he was wanted in the principal's office, all the kids went, "Woooooo!" The Shark didn't say a word. He just glared and gave me a swift kick as he walked past my desk.

He didn't come back during fourth period, and he never showed up for P.E. class, so it wasn't until after school that I found out what happened.

Logan and I were waiting for his dad again in the parking lot when The Shark, his teeth bared, came skidding up on his bike. He leapt off, threw his bike on the ground, and grabbed me by the collar.

"I'd like to smash you like a potato chip," he growled. "I'd like to twist you like a pretzel. I'd like to fry you like bacon. I'd like to — "

"I get your meaning," I said, trying to loosen his grip. My heart was pounding in my throat.

"Gee, why am I so hungry all of a sudden?" Logan remarked.

"Shut up!" The Shark said. He released my collar with such fierceness that I almost fell over. "I'd like to grind you like hamburger, Weirdo. But if I hurt you on school property, I'll just be in worse trouble." He started jabbing my chest with a sharp finger. "You got me suspended today, Weirdo. You and your wimpy squealings to Wesley and Curtis. Now I'm out of here for a month, *and* my dad will probably send me to that stupid disciplinary school for the rest of the year."

"That's not my problem," I said coolly.

"Wanna bet? You're gonna pay for this."

Just then I heard the opening notes to the Winnie-the-Pooh song. Logan's dad must've gotten tied up, because the Heffalump pulled alongside the curb.

Oh, man, what rotten timing. I could feel my cheeks starting to ignite.

"Over here, Rob!" Mom called gaily from the window, as if I wouldn't have noticed. Winnie sat beside her. She waved, but I looked away.

"Let's go," I said to Logan.

"I haven't excused you yet." The Shark spoke through clenched teeth. "You're safe now, Weirdo, with Mommy and Baby Sis hanging around. But just wait. The next time you take one step off school property alone, I'll be there. Are you listening, Weirdo? I'm gonna get you and I'm gonna get you *bad*. That's a promise."

With one last, sharp finger-jab to my chest, The Shark whirled to pick up his bike. He pulled a wheelie, then spun out of the parking lot. I just stood there, limp and numb, watching him go.

Logan thumped me on the back. "Don't worry, Rob. I won't let you walk off this campus alone. Besides, I've seen *The Karate Kid* twenty-eight times. By now I probably know enough karate moves to be registered as a human lethal weapon." He hopped around, hands slashing at the air. "Yessiree. In three seconds, I could turn The Shark into sushi. Don't you worry."

"Yeah, okay," I said, but my voice sounded hollow. I knew I couldn't spend the rest of my life using my family and friends as bodyguards. I also knew The Shark better than to take his threats lightly. He meant what he'd said. And his last words continued to echo in my mind all the rest of that week: *I'm gonna get you and I'm gonna get you bad. That's a promise.*

SIXTEEN

The Shark kept his word. Every morning and every afternoon I saw him lounging just outside the school gates. Sometimes he was sharpening a pencil with his teeth. Sometimes he was chanting *weirdo, weirdo, weirdo* in a low whisper. Sometimes I wouldn't see him at all, just his bike leaning against the fence. But I knew he was around somewhere, waiting. Waiting to catch me alone . . .

Logan also kept his word. He stuck to me like Superglue, often pulling me into a cluster of other kids as they entered campus. But that didn't stop me from feeling The Shark's eyes, cold and black and depthless, from boring into the back of my head as I hurried past.

Although The Shark was out of my life the rest of the time, I still had to suffer the repercussions of Winnie. Kids teased me every day. Newspaper and TV reporters showed up on our doorstep at all hours, trying to get the latest scoop. The phone rang constantly. Piglet howled frequently. And Mom's book business boomed. I guess people thought it was neat to buy stuff from the mother of the famous Winnie.

I saw Jenner a few of times in the halls at school, but I managed to avoid her. Once she was even waiting outside of Wesley's class. When she saw me she opened her mouth, like she was about to say something. "I'm late!" I cried, interrupting her, and dashed into the boys' rest room. I stayed there, washing my hands about forty times, until the next bell rang. I didn't want to hear what Jenner had to say. I didn't want to hear those painful words: *I'm sorry, Rob, but I can't go to any more* Star Trek *movies with a weirdo like you.*

One good thing happened that week: Bill from Bike and Skate *finally* fixed my BMX. But even that was tainted by Winnie. When I went to pick up my bike, Bill handed me a slightly mangled candy bar.

"Give this to the kid genius, you hear?" he said. "I've been readin' all about her. Make sure you tell her this treat is from her old pal, Uncle Bill."

Uncle Bill! I could've gagged, but Winnie seemed pleased. She wolfed down the chocolate in about three seconds. "Thanks," she said softly. Then she stared at me with those sad, brown-bear eyes, like she was waiting for something else.

I gazed back at her. For a second, I felt words

struggling to get out of my throat. Words of pride. I wanted to hug her and say, *Well done, Winnie. Look what you've accomplished!* But then I remembered the embarrassing articles, and the teasing and giggling at school, and the way The Shark had spit out the name *Weirdo*.

I turned away without saying a word.

I woke up the following Monday with the creepy feeling that someone was watching me.

I opened my eye a crack. Steve was playing vulture on my chest, gazing down at me with his wide, unblinking gold eyes.

"You haven't done this in a long time," I said, stroking him behind the ears. "Are you trying to send me a special cat message or something? You know, like Lassie used to do in those old TV shows?"

I nudged him over a bit so I could breathe. "Let's see, one meow could mean, *Excuse me, Rob, but the house is on fire.* Two meows could mean, *Quick, hide under the table. I feel an earthquake coming on.* And three meows would mean — "

"Meowmeowmeow," Steve said.

"Oh, no," I cried. "I completely forgot! It's *Career Day*."

Someone knocked on the door.

Before I could answer, Dad burst in.

"Good morning!" he sang. He wore baggy shorts, a Hawaiian shirt (untucked), and his flip-flops. "Guess what day it is?"

I pulled the covers over my head. "The day my life is over."

He made a sound like a game show buzzer. "Wrong!"

"I hope you're going to tell me it's the day we're moving to Outer Mongolia. That's the only answer I'll accept."

"Wrong again," Dad said. "It's the day your old man is gonna wow the students of Jefferson Junior High with his wild and gnarly surf stories."

I peeked over the top of my blanket. "Promise me one thing, Dad. Promise me you won't show off your fake great white shark scar."

Dad ignored me. "Let's see, the assembly starts at one o'clock, so why don't we meet in front of the school around twelve-thirty? You can help me carry in my boards and the slide projector. Oh, and it'll be all right if Winnie sits with you, won't it?"

I sat bolt upright, knocking Steve off the bed. "Winnie? *Winnie's* coming with you?"

"Righty-o," Dad said. "Mom has an all-day meeting, and Winnie gets out of school at noon, so I'll need to bring her along."

I moaned. "Can't you get a baby-sitter? I mean, there's no way I can be seen at the first junior high assembly sitting next to my five-year-old sister!"

"You'll just have to wear a paper bag over your head, won't you?" Dad replied. "Besides, since you two won't get together willingly these days, it's up to me to force the issue."

"I don't think it's a good idea having Winnie at the assembly," I said, trying a different approach. "It's gonna be a long one, and you're not the only parent who's speaking. What if Winnie gets bored?"

"She won't get bored. Not when she sees the

radical slides I'm bringing." He moved to leave.

"Wait a minute!" I cried. "You're not going to show any slides of *me*, are you?"

"Just wait and see," Dad said with a wink and a laugh.

I buried under the blankets again. I wondered if there could possibly be anyone left at school who didn't know me as the Seventh-Grade Weirdo. If so, Dad and Winnie's visit would certainly take care of that by two o'clock this afternoon.

"There's your dad," Logan said, nudging me in the ribs. It was twelve-thirty, and we were standing on the front steps of the school. Dad's van had just sputtered around the corner and gasped to a stop. He opened the door.

"Oh, no," I squeaked. "He's wearing his wet suit! Logan, my dad's going to go on stage wearing his *wet suit*."

Logan put on his sunglasses. "Whoa, that thing's bright, man! Quick, let's help him carry in his stuff before we're seen. I think everybody's still in the cafeteria." He started down the steps.

"Wait!" I hissed, grabbing his arm. "The Shark's down there."

"Where?"

I pointed. "There, behind that tree. See his blond hair?" A chill prickled my neck. "He must stand out here all day, in case I try to sneak by."

"Well, what did you think," Logan said, "that he had regular hours like a school crossing guard? Come on, let's help your dad."

I didn't move. "What about The Shark?"

"He's not going to do anything to you with your dad around, so come *on*."

I followed Logan across the street, keeping my eyes straight ahead. I knew you-know-who was watching.

"Hello, boys," Dad said.

"Uh, aren't you a little hot in your wet suit?" I asked hopefully.

"Nope. Feel great! Logan, grab that slide projector, will you? Rob, hold Winnie's hand, please. No, no, I'll carry the boards."

"Man, look at the size of 'em," Logan said, watching as Dad pulled two sleek longboards from the back of the van. "You could go bowling on those things."

"Just about," Dad laughed. "These are called elephant guns. They're the only surfboards big enough to handle the gnarly thirty-footers at Waimea. Okay, lead the way."

We crossed the street, Logan lugging the projector, Dad padding along in his bare feet, a board under each arm. Winnie trotted beside me. The Shark was now standing just outside the school gate. Unconsciously, I tightened my grip on Winnie's hand.

"Ouch," she said.

"Sorry," I replied, but I didn't let go.

Out of the corner of my eye, I could see The Shark staring at us. Under his breath he taunted, "Weirdo, weirdo, weirdo."

Frowning, Winnie stared back at him, looking over her shoulder as we passed.

"Who's that little hoodlum?" Dad asked, just

loud enough for The Shark to hear. "The leader of the local snowman gang?" He chuckled at his own joke. I thought I heard The Shark hiss.

"He's nobody," I said, quickening my pace. I tugged at Winnie's hand. She was still staring over her shoulder.

Once inside the school, I showed Dad how to get to the booth above the back of the auditorium. Someone from the A.V. department was going to help him set up and run his slide projector from there. Then we went backstage where Mr. Wesley and the four other Career Day parents were waiting. Their kids were there, too. They didn't seem any happier about this whole thing than I was, but that didn't stop them from snorting and giggling about Dad. Especially when he and Wesley hugged each other and started doing all sorts of bizarre surfer handshakes.

"Get a load of that getup," one guy said, thumbing at Dad's Day-Glo outfit.

"Is that a weight-reducing suit, or what?" said another guy.

A girl chomping a wad of juicy gum glanced at Winnie. "Who's this," she asked, "your date?"

The guys snickered.

An eighth-grade girl I'd seen hanging around The Shark said, "Hey, I know you. You're the Seventh-Grade Weirdo. And this must be your genius sister, the Kindergarten Weirdo!"

More snickering.

"You're very observant," Winnie said softly, "for a person with the brains of a toothbrush."

The girl bristled. (No pun intended.)

"Uh, Logan, maybe we'd better find a place to sit now," I said. "It's almost one o'clock. Come on, Winnie." I gave her a push. The sooner she was hidden in a far, dark seat, the better.

Dad called after us. "Don't forget to root for your old man, all right, Rob?"

Yeah, I'd be rooting for him all right. From where I'd be hiding at the bottom of my bookpack.

Logan and I chose seats in the back row of the auditorium. I made Winnie sit on the aisle. Who knows what kind of trouble she'd get me into if she was sitting next to some kid.

The auditorium started to fill. Kids took their seats, laughing and shoving, throwing pencils or snapping rubber bands at each other.

"He doesn't like you very much, does he?" Winnie said in a solemn voice.

"Who doesn't?" I asked absently. I was measuring my bookpack with my hands, trying to figure if I'd have to take the books out before my head would fit in it.

"The boy with the white hair," Winnie went on. "Mr. Shark. He's always mean to you."

"You got that right," I said.

"Why was he calling you a weirdo?"

I gazed pointedly at her. "I wonder."

Winnie didn't answer. She looked down at her hands, folded neatly in her lap.

After a pause, she said, "Rob, why was he standing outside? Doesn't he go to school?"

"He got kicked out of school. He thinks it's my fault, so now he hangs around every day, waiting to be even meaner to me. Hey, Logan, let me see your bookpack for a second. Is it bigger than mine?"

"That's bad," Winnie said. "Someone should wash his mouth out with soap. Someone should give him a lecture."

"Uh-huh. You have to be quiet now, Winnie. The assembly's gonna start."

The lights eased low. Winnie wiggled around, getting up on her knees so she could see over the kid in front of her. The curtains opened, and everyone started to clap. A spotlight shone down on Mr. Wesley and the five parents seated in chairs on stage. The audience started to crack up when they noticed Dad in his wet suit. Oblivious, he grinned and waved.

I hunkered down in my seat.

Mr. Wesley started introducing the parents. There were two moms, a stockbroker and a medical technologist, and two dads, an engineer and a mechanic. All normal jobs. All normal people. All except Dad.

The stockbroker went first. She'd been talking for a while before I noticed Jenner, making her way slowly up the aisle. She craned her neck, scanning each row, as if looking for someone.

Me.

I hunched lower in my seat, trying to make myself invisible.

"Isn't that your friend?" Winnie asked in a loud voice.

"No," I whispered, "I don't have any friends."

"Yes, you do. It's Jenner. I like Jenner. So did Kanga."

"It's not Jenner," I said. I was now hunched so low, I was almost flat on my back.

"It looks like Jenner."

"I know. That's because, uh, because it's her twin sister . . . Henner."

"Oh."

"Be quiet now," I said.

Too late.

"Hi, Henner!" Winnie called.

Why is there never a good earthquake when you need one?

"Winnie, hi!" Jenner said in a hoarse whisper. "And Rob — there you are! I've been looking all over for you. Rob, we have to talk. Now." She pulled my arm, half lifting me out of my seat.

"Uh, we can't talk now," I said.

"Why not?" she demanded.

"Because there's an assembly going on. Besides, I'm supposed to be watching Winnie."

"Logan can watch me," Winnie replied. "Can't you, Logan?"

"Yeah, yeah, sure." He was taking notes in a little pad of paper. "Now be quiet, will you? I'm trying to learn about mutual funds."

The kid in front of us turned around and said, "SHHHH!"

"Sorry," Jenner said. "Let's go, Rob. We'll be right back, Winnie."

"Where are we going?" I asked once we'd exited the auditorium.

"Up to the booth. I'm supposed to keep an eye on your dad's slide projector during his talk. We'd better hurry. He'll be on second."

We climbed the stairs to the darkened booth. A guy at the end of the room was monitoring the spotlights.

Jenner started to adjust Dad's projector. "I want to know," she began, "why you've been avoiding me all week."

"I haven't been —"

"Yes, you have. And I want to know why. Did I do something again to make you mad? Don't you like me?"

I stood staring down into her green eyes. My cheeks got hot. I glanced at the spotlight guy, but he didn't seem aware of us. "Uh, actually," I mumbled, "I like you very much."

Jenner didn't answer. Mr. Wesley had introduced Dad. The audience was cracking up again.

"Cowabunga, dudes!" Dad's voice boomed over the P.A. The audience laughed harder. I knew my cheeks were glowing as red as his wet suit.

"I'm here to tell you about the life of a pro surfer," Dad's voice struggled over the laughter. "You won't ever get rich in this job — you'll need a college degree to help you with that. The hours are grueling, and the training is never-ending, but you *will* get a chance to catch some of the most awesome waves around the world. Could the A.V. person switch on my projector, please?"

The auditorium darkened even more. Jenner flipped on the projector, setting the controls on automatic. Dad's slides would now click on and off every couple of seconds.

"Sorry," Jenner said, smiling. "Duty calls, you know. Now, what was it you said?"

"Uh, nothing. Nothing."

"No, you said something, I just didn't hear what. Tell me, Rob."

I cleared my throat. "I said that I, uh, like you very much."

Jenner crossed her arms. "Well. You certainly have a funny way of showing it. Hey, don't you want to sit down?"

I would've sold my BMX for the chance to sit next to her again! I sat.

"I like you, too, Rob," she said. "A lot."

"You don't think I'm —" I paused. "You don't think I'm weird?"

She thought that over for a second. "Weird. I don't think so. Maybe I don't know you well enough yet. Do you get worse?"

"Yes. No. I mean . . ."

Jenner laughed. "Rob, I'm teasing. I don't think you're weird at all. And I don't understand why The Shark was calling you the Seventh-Grade Weirdo. You seem like a perfectly normal person to me."

A balloon of happiness swelled inside my chest. "I'm normal? You think I'm normal? And that's why you like me?"

Jenner fidgeted for a moment. "Well, no. I mean, everyone I know is normal. And that's so *boring*. But when I heard you give that Patrick Henry speech the other day, I realized there's something more inside you that I haven't seen yet."

"So you don't think that I'm . . . or that my family or Winnie is . . ."

"I think you're *extraordinary*," Jenner proclaimed. "Yes, that's it. Extraordinary. Like people in a movie. Or a book. You know, stories where people do unusual things. Stories with happy endings. Know what I mean?"

I wasn't sure I did. But it didn't matter. Despite Winnie's weirdness, and my family's weirdness, Jenner still liked me!

"Who thinks your family is weird?" Jenner demanded. "Besides The Shark, that is. I mean, I think Winnie is sweet. Your mom and dad seem nice, too. Who would think anything else?"

I waved my hand toward the audience. "They would. They do. Just listen to them laugh."

"Huh. Who *cares* what they think? And in case you haven't noticed, they're *not* laughing."

"Oh, sure. Just listen — "

I stopped.

Jenner was right.

They weren't laughing.

They were cheering. They were hooting. They were even *listening*. But they weren't laughing.

Dad's slides clicked away. I leaned forward, looking through the booth glass, down into the audience.

"They like him," I said, half to myself. "They actually *like* him!"

"Even if they didn't, it wouldn't matter to me at all," Jenner said.

I looked at her. The slides clicked one by one. Light, dark. Light, dark. Jenner's eyes seemed to spark with each one. I liked that fire behind them.

I reached over and grasped her hand.

"I hope . . . I hope I didn't hurt your feelings this week," I said, the words coming slow. "I was afraid to talk to you, afraid you wouldn't want to be my friend anymore."

"I'll always be your friend." Jenner's fingers felt warm and firm as they squeezed mine. Her lips curved up in that special smile. The smile meant only for me. I could smell her hair. Summer and peaches. I leaned toward her . . .

The audience broke into thunderous applause. Jenner and I both jumped.

"Thank you very much, Mr. Robin," I heard Mr. Wesley say over cheers and whistles. "Jenner? Are you up there? You can turn off the projector. Thank you. And now, our next guest . . ."

"I guess I'd better get back to Winnie," I said, not really wanting to. I wanted to stay in this little darkened room and hold Jenner's hand for the next sixty-eight years.

"Okay," she answered. "I'm all finished here. Mind if I sit with you?"

"There aren't any empty seats in our row."

"That's okay. Maybe Winnie could sit in my lap."

"Sure," I said.

We made our way back downstairs. I took her hand again as we entered the darkened auditorium. It suddenly seemed the easiest and most natural thing in the world.

"Hey, Logan," I whispered. "Where's Winnie?" Her seat was empty.

He shrugged. "I don't know. She was here a minute ago. Man, your dad was fantastic!"

The kid in front of him whirled around. "That was *your* dad?" he asked, incredulous.

I nodded.

"Cool. Those waves he was riding were gnarly! Your dad can really thrash."

"Thanks," I said, filling with pride. Then I remembered Winnie. I searched under her seat. Nothing there but a few petrified pieces of bubble gum.

"Logan," I whispered. "You were supposed to keep an eye on her. Now where is she?"

"I told you, I don't know. And don't get mad at me. She's *your* sister."

"I'm not mad. I've just gotta find her."

"She must be around someplace," Jenner said. "Maybe she went to the bathroom."

"That's it," Logan said. "When the broker finished talking, Winnie was kind of wiggling around. Maybe she had to pee." He snapped his fingers. "Oh, yeah! She said something about soap."

"I'll check the girls' rest room," Jenner offered, and slipped out the door.

"Did she actually tell you she had to use the bathroom?" I asked.

"Well, no," Logan admitted. "But then, I wasn't really listening. I heard her mumbling about washing her mouth out with soap. That's weird, huh? I wonder why she'd want to do that?"

A faint alarm sounded in the back of my mind.

Soap. When had Winnie been talking about . . . ?

The alarm clanged louder. And then I remembered.

Winnie had wanted to wash The Shark's mouth out with soap!

I'm gonna get you and I'm gonna get you bad. That's a promise.

SEVENTEEN

I felt cold all over. As cold as the day I'd fallen into Jenner's swimming pool.

Winnie. My sister. Alone with The Shark.

I shook my head as if to dispel the thought. Maybe I was wrong. Oh, let me be wrong. She wouldn't *really* try to wash The Shark's mouth out with soap.

Would she?

No. Not even Winnie was that weird. But she might try to talk to him. Especially if she thought that would fix things between him and me. And between me and her.

I raced out of the auditorium, colliding with Jenner.

"Was she in there?" I asked. "In the bathroom?"

"No. What's the matter?"

"I think Winnie's with The Shark."

"The Shark! What's she doing with him?"

I started to jog down the hall. "He'd better not hurt her. If he does, it's my fault. *My* fault."

"What are you talking about, Rob? What's going on? How can it be your fault?"

I didn't answer. I thought back to the first time I had ever seen The Shark. His eyes. I remember how they'd made me mad, and how I wanted to stare back at them the same way he stared at me. But I didn't. I'd wimped out. Played it safe. And I'd been doing that ever since.

I glanced at Jenner, keeping pace beside me. The thought of Winnie with The Shark must've made her cold, too. She was rubbing the goose bumps on her arms, like the day I'd pretended to be Patrick Henry.

I halted. "It's just like the speech," I said.

"What speech?"

"The Revolutionary War," I continued, half talking to myself. I started jogging again, toward the main doors of the school. "It's like what we've been learning about in class. Some people — Americans — didn't want to fight. They wanted to keep things peaceful and safe, you know? But they didn't have any freedom that way."

"What does that have to do with Winnie? And The Shark?" Jenner asked.

I didn't answer. We had reached the main doors. I peeked through the panes. The Shark lounged just outside the school gates. He towered over Winnie, who stood shaking a finger at him.

Someone should give him a lecture.

I might've laughed — if I hadn't been so scared.

"Go back to the assembly," I told Jenner.

"No, I want to go with you." Her voice sounded nervous.

"I'll be okay." I swallowed at a lump in my throat. "I'll be back in a minute. I just have to get Winnie."

I took a deep breath. Then, without looking back, I pushed open the doors and headed down the walkway. I kept my back as straight as I could, head high. I didn't want The Shark to notice that my knees were quivering like Jell-O.

"Well, look who's here," The Shark sneered when I reached the chainlink fence. "The Seventh-Grade Weirdo himself. Little Miss Winnie-the-Pooh has been telling me that I've been 'mean' to you. Poor, poor Weirdo. You really have it rough."

I ignored him, and stopped just this side of the gate. "Come here, Winnie. We need to go back inside. Dad's waiting."

"Not yet," Winnie said. "Mr. Shark hasn't promised."

"Hasn't promised what?" I asked.

"She wants me to stop being mean to you, Weirdo." The Shark laughed. "You don't have the guts to walk through that gate and ask me youself. You don't have the guts to take your punishment. So you send your midget sister to do your dirty work instead. What a wimp."

Winnie put her hands on her hips. "You're being mean again," she warned.

"And what are you gonna do about it?" The Shark demanded."Kick me in the ankle? Hit me in the foot with your teddy bear? Ooo, I'm scared. I'm shakin'!"

I gripped the fence. "Leave her alone."

"Make me."

"Winnie," I began, "come back inside the gate now, okay? It's not going to do any good talking to this guy. Just come back inside."

"I want him to stop," Winnie said. "I want him to stop so you won't be mad at me anymore."

My heart gave a squeeze. Tears pricked my eyes. "I'm not mad at you, Winnie."

"Yes, you are. You said so."

"You're right. I did say that. But I'm not mad anymore. Honest, Winnie. Really and truly I'm not."

Winnie blinked. Suddenly she looked very small and helpless. "All right," she said at last and took a step forward.

The Shark grabbed her sleeve.

"Hey!" Winnie said.

"Not so fast." The Shark tugged her back. "Weirdo, if you want Baby Sis, you gotta come out here and get her."

Okay. That's easy, I told myself. Just open the gate. Take those few steps . . .

I couldn't move.

My words came out a croak. "Let go of her."

The evil smile. "No."

Winnie struggled, but The Shark held fast. "Let go," she said. Her lip trembled.

Anger welled in my stomach. It felt like a hard ball of flame. Still, I couldn't move.

"Let her go, Mike," I said. "Let her go *now*."

"You come and get her."

The fence still stood between us. It seemed higher than before. I felt trapped, imprisoned.

"This is the last time I'm asking nice, Mike. *Let my sister go*."

"No."

"Let *go*!" Winnie repeated. She yanked free, her shirt sleeve slipping through Mike's fingers. She fell, skinning her knee. When she looked up, I saw tears in her eyes.

The flame inside me turned white-hot. *My sister. He'd hurt my sister.*

"Give me liberty, or give me death!" I shouted. I flung open the gate and charged into Mike. Without thinking, I grabbed him by the collar and slammed him against the fence. I felt crazy. Mad crazy. "I asked you" — I shouted — "to leave my — sister — *alone*!" With a Ninja cry, I hauled back and kicked the fence as hard as I could. The crash vibrated in my head, and I saw Mike flinch.

He reached out to grab me, but I was too fast. I gathered more T-shirt into my fist and pulled him closer, our noses almost touching. I could feel his breath on my face. I stared straight into his eyes.

And that's when I saw something. Something I hadn't noticed before.

Mike's eyes weren't really black. They were dark brown. And they stared back at me like regular eyes.

No laser beams.

No bottomless pits.

Just eyes.

Maybe it was my imagination, but I thought I saw a tremor, just a tiny tremor of fear in those eyes.

He's not so tough, I thought. And maybe he never had been. I'd thought he was powerful, but I was the one who gave him that power. He'd made fun of my family, and I let him. He'd called me a weirdo, and I believed him. I'd made him more important than my own family. More important than myself.

"Let go of me," Mike said, his words distant, unsure. "Or . . . or I'll tell everyone at school that you've been crying and blubbering about your baby sister."

"Who cares?" I said. I knew I didn't.

Shrugging, I let go of his shirt. He slumped against the fence. I turned and hurried to where Winnie had fallen. I knelt beside her. She looked at me and blinked.

"Thank you, Gandalf," she said softly.

"You're welcome, Bilbo," I answered and gathered her into my arms.

The End

Winnie's game Once Upon a Time hit the stores right before Christmas, and have been selling like crazy ever since. Winnie is so rich, she could fill a room with money and jump around in it like Scrooge McDuck, but so far she still likes reading and thinking the best. She already has an idea for a new game. It's called Shark Bite.

Logan joined seventeen clubs that semester, just so he could be close to Gabriela, who has a lot of school spirit. He even tried out for cheerleader, dressed in a wig and short skirt, but Gabriela caught on. I think his hairy legs gave him away. Gabriela's dating a high school guy now, but Logan still believes she has B.D.s (Burning Desires) for him.

Yeah, it's true — some of my best friends are weirdos.

On our American history project, Logan, Gabriela, and I got A's! Mr. Wesley said it was the most creative presentation he'd ever seen. Jenner said it gave her goose bumps.

Jenner. Beautiful, green-eyed Jenner. She's a ninth-grader now and goes to high school. But it doesn't bother her one bit having a boyfriend who's still in junior high.

I never saw The Shark again. I hope I never do. I heard that his family moved out of town, so beware. He might be cruising the halls of *your* school.

As for me, well, I know that I'll never have a normal, ordinary family. But then, what's wrong with being extraordinary? Jenner made me realize that. We're like people in a book. People you like to read about, people who do extraordinary things. It doesn't matter if the kids at school think we're weirdos. It only matters what *I* think. And I think we're gonna live happily ever after.

About the Author

Lee Wardlaw is a former teacher and the author of several books for young readers. She enjoys bodysurfing, talking on the phone, chewing bubble gum, and wearing hats. Lee lives in Santa Barbara, California, with her husband and their two cats — weirdos all, and proud of it.